I0654613

GATHER THE PARTY

ANTONY SOEHNER

5 Prince Publishing

GATHER THE PARTY

Antony Soehner

5 PRINCE PUBLISHING & BOOKS, LLC

PO Box 16507, Denver, CO 80216

www.5PrinceBooks.com

Digital:ISBN-10:1-63112-200-2, ISBN-13:978-1-63112-200-2

Print: ISBN-10:1-63112-201-0 ISBN-13:978-1-63112-201-9

GATHER THE PARTY. Antony Soehner

Copyright ANTONY SOEHNER 2017

Published by 5 Prince Publishing

Cover Credit: Joshua Stolte

Author Photo Credit: Brenden Murphy

First Edition 2017

To my Parents,
who told me to go turn my hobby into a lifestyle!

ACKNOWLEDGMENTS

Thank you Joshua Stolte for guiding me through this world of geeky-ness, and helping me find my love and passion for Dungeons and Dragons, as well as everything else along the way! MTFBWY

All my family and friends, the cast of Critical Role, and the awesome people over at Wizards of the Coast who helped me get this book going.

GATHER THE PARTY

Antony Soehner

AN EXPECTED PARTY

I stared out the car window the whole drive. I was getting into my mental space, remembering every little thing I knew about my character. I did this every Friday night on the drive over to Liam's uncle's house.

I started through my mental stat sheet to make sure all my notes were up to date: Adrik Frostbeard, Level 10 Dwarf Barbarian. Max Hit points: 105. Current Hit Points: 95. We kinda got jumped at the last session by a band of goblins. I ran along my stats on the left of my page. I chuckle every time I see my 19 strength score followed by my eight charisma score. Imagine little me going into combat as Adrik does. I wouldn't even be able to lift my great axe.

We're here! That fifteen-minute drive always flies by when I'm getting focused.

"Come on, Mom! Unlock the door!" I excitedly shouted at my mom. She always smiles from ear to ear when I try to tuck and roll out of the moving car.

"Calm down, sweetheart," she said, as she turned the car into the driveway. "You know I'll never let you get out of the moving car. And you also know that I'm coming in to say hi and pay for your part of the pizza. Can't just let Liam's uncle feed my human trash compactor." Mom always reminds me how much I eat when we pull up. I can't help it. I'm always hungry! What kid isn't?

"Come on, Mom! Stop the car!" I shouted again. I was practically hanging halfway out the window of the car trying to escape the cage my mom had me in.

"Jack, you'll be ok. We're the first ones here... like always. You guys don't ever start on time anyway. Remind me again, why do we always have to be here forty-five minutes early?" Mom asked like she always did. She knows the answer. You can see it in her smile.

"You know why, Mom," I sighed to her. "Me and Liam—"

"Liam and I," she interrupted.

"Whatever. Liam and I. Better?" I asked sarcastically, rolling my eyes so far into my head I started seeing stars... you know like when you rub your eyes a little too hard?

"Better." She laughed at me. She could see how excited I was to get out.

"Liam and I like to read through Chris Perkins' tweets and listen to 'Dragon Talk'. We wanna learn what's new and coming up at Wizards of the Coast!" I exclaimed for probably the zillionth time this month. She always asks me so she can stall to count out the cash to give to Liam's uncle. But she loves how passionate I am about this.

"Oh right," she said through her massive grin. "And Chris Perkins, he's that guy we watch on the internet on Thursday nights, right?"

"Oh my god, Mom! No!" I knew she was just messing with me now, she watches the show with me. "That's Matt Mercer!" I crossed my eyes at her to show her how annoyed I was getting.

"Ok, ok, Mr. Know-it-all. Let's go inside. Do you have all the stuff you need? Dice?"

"Got it!"

"Pencils and pens?"

"Right here!" I held out the hundreds of pencils in my pencil bag.

"Inhaler?" She looked at me sternly with that mom stare that peers into your soul.

"Yup," I lied to her, trying not to make eye contact.

"Show it to me," she said. Her gaze is now burning into my heart. I knew she could see right through my lies. I could feel it in her stare.

"Ok, no. I forgot it at home again," I lied to her again. I didn't forget it. I left it at home. I don't need it anymore. You have one asthma attack because you got a little too excited playing, and all of a sudden you're gonna die if you don't take it with you. She reached into her purse and took out the little red inhaler with my name written on the side.

"Take it." Now her evil mom glare has turned into a loving, worried mother stare. "I know you don't like having it, but I want to make sure you're safe. You know what Papa always tells you, right?"

"Better safe than sorry," I sighed out. Papa is my grandpa on my mom's side. When he was younger, he almost died because he didn't have an inhaler. So now because of that, I always have to carry mine. Finally, we got out of the car. I threw one strap of my super heavy backpack over my shoulder and booked it to the front door. I didn't even make it to the porch when I heard Liam's uncle's phone doing that doorbell jingle that alerts him someone is at the door. By the time I reach the door, Liam and his uncle are there.

"Come on, Jack! I've got the podcast loaded and ready to go! We gotta hurry! The rest of them are gonna be here any minute now!" Liam shouted. He turned to run into the house, but before he could take a step, his uncle wheeled his chair behind him to block his path.

"Why don't you let Jack say goodbye to his mom?" His uncle softly reminded him.

"I guess you're right. Sorry, Uncle Matt. Jack, make sure to tell your mom goodbye," Liam said, embarrassed and somber. "But make it quick, they'll be here soon." And without missing a beat, Liam bolted up the stairs in a blur.

"Thanks, Matt. Oh, and here," Mom pulled out the money she'd taken from her wallet earlier, "for the pizza. And don't tell me not to worry about it. I know my son eats more pizza than all the other kiddos combined. It's the least I can do for what you're doing," she lectured, and held the money out in front of her.

"You know I can't take that. It's my treat. Plus, if Jack here didn't eat as much as he does, I would probably still have pizza from a year ago. The kid is a life saver. And he's such a good kid." Mr. R has always been such a nice guy like that. He hardly ever takes the money from the parents.

"Well, then think of it as babysitting money, since you take so much time out of your Friday nights to watch and hang out with the kids. Please, Matt, just take this. I'll make plenty of tips tonight. It's just a small token of appreciation," Mom says, very soft and sweet. She reached down and took Mr. R's hand, and placed the money in his palm. I rolled my eyes again at my mom. She's taking too long!

"Alright, alright. Thank you, Jess. I appreciate it. Now I'll let you guys say goodbye. Liam is gonna lose it if I keep you any longer," he said, looking up towards Liam's bedroom. He wheeled himself back into the house and towards the kitchen.

"Ok, Jackie, go have fun tonight. Kill me a dragon? I hear their scales shine brighter than diamonds," she joked, as she squeezed me with a big hug and a large kiss on the forehead. "I love you, kiddo. You have no idea how much." She squeezed me a little tighter before letting me go.

"Love you too, Mama," I say with a bit of hesitance, making sure no one heard me. "Be safe at work tonight. Beat up a few drunks for me? I hear their teeth are yellower than sunflowers." We both chuckled at that one. "Bye, Mom! Love you,' I exclaimed before I kissed her cheek and turned into the house.

"Not too much soda tonight, OK?" she hollered into the house before closing the door.

"Yes, Ma'am," I sighed out again.

"See you boys at one o'clock!" she yelled. The front door clicked shut. I started my run up the stairs but just then. .

"Hey, Jack, before you go upstairs, come see me in the kitchen," Mr. R called out. As soon as those words reached my ears, I started going through everything I did this week. Why would he wanna see me in the kitchen? Did my principal call him about my grades instead of mom? Did I get caught at school when I went into the girls' bathroom by accident? I could've sworn nobody saw me! Oh god, what did I do? I went back down the stairs and into the kitchen.

"What's up, Mr. Rollins? Everything okay?" I'm trying to stay calm. Maybe nothing's wrong. But if I show I'm worried, he's gonna know something's up. I could feel the cold sweat beading on my brow.

"Oh yeah, everything is perfect. Just wanted to see what pizza you wanted." He always asks what kind of pizza I eat, and it's always the same.

"You know me, Mr. Rollins. I'll eat anything you give me. But I'm a sucker for sausage, green pepper, and mushroom. Just like my Grandpa," I said with a smile. All the tension dropped off my back. I'm not in trouble after all. I turned to walk away, but before I can even take a step...

"Oh, one more thing before you get too far." His tone has

changed. It's a bit more stern and parent-like. I started sweating again. If I turn around is he going to have that soul-burning mom stare too? "I want you to hold on to this." I turned around to see him holding out some cash. My mom's cash. "Your mom is sweet, but I don't need babysitting money. You're more of an adult than I am some days. Will you sneak it back into her wallet when you guys go home?" He extended his arm and leaned a bit away from his chair to hand me the money so I could take it without hitting my shins on the feet-support things on his chair.

"Oh yeah, I gotcha, Mr. Rollins. Anything for you." The tension dropped again from my back, like a trillion elephants were taken off my neck.

"Jack! Are you coming or what? We're not going to get to finish Dragon Talk if you keep lollygagging!" Liam shouted down the stairs. I start running to the stairs, and I look back to catch Mr. Rollins take his hand from his chin to his lap. I caught the *thank you* in sign language and signed back to him, *you're welcome*.

I ran up the stairs faster than Wally West and exploded into Liam's room, landing in the massive maroon Lovesac next to him.

"Took you long enough," Liam blurted out, "Did you tell your mommy you wuv her?"

"Oh, shut up and start it! They're gonna be here any minute!" I mimicked Liam just to see his eyes roll.

"No shit, Sherlock!" Liam whispered. He looked out the door to make sure his uncle didn't hear him swear.

"What are you looking for? He's downstairs on the phone ordering pizza. Start the freaking podcast already!" I exclaimed jokingly to Liam. And as I was expecting, Liam threw a solid punch into my shoulder. I was already braced for it and watched him pull away, flicking his hand in pain.

"Ow! You can't flex when you know I'm gonna hit you! That's

cheating," Liam complained. But what was I supposed to do? He hits me every time I pick on him. I know it's coming. I'm not just gonna make it easy on him.

"Would you just start the podcast already?" Right as I asked, the doorbell rang.

"Now look what you've done! Now we have to wait 'til next week to hear Chris and Matt talk about new lore," Liam whined. This time he punched me before I was ready. This one really hurt. I think they call this a dead arm.

Liam and I went racing down the stairs, pushing and shoving each other. Ultimately getting beat to the door by his uncle.

"Slow down, slow down. You're both gonna hurt yourselves one of these days coming down those stairs like that." Mr. R seemed to always think we were going to hurt ourselves. I guess he's not wrong. We did once have to cancel our game night to take Liam and I both to the hospital to check for concussions after we both fell down the stairs. But I mean, what are the odds that we would do that again?

Mr. R unlocked the door and wheeled back to open it. And there on the porch was Daryl.

"Daryl! Are you actually early? What happened? Did you forget to not wear a watch today?" Liam joked. You could see there was excitement on Daryl's face. And I knew exactly what had happened. He gets this stupid smile every few months. And it could only mean one thing!

"You have that stupid look on your face, Daryl. What did you get this time?" I shouted as I ran at him to see.

"Jack, let Daryl come in first before you start tearing his bag apart again," Mr. R said. "Daryl, it's good to see ya, buddy. Did you have a safe ride over here?" Daryl always rides his bike over here because he only lives in the neighborhood. But because he never leaves until game time, he's always late.

"I didn't ride here tonight, Mr. Rollins," Daryl said with a huge smile on his face.

"Really? Then how did you get here? Did your mom get the night off?" Liam's uncle looked puzzled. Daryl's mom works at the local 7/11. She always gets stuck with the night shift and then tries to double shift to earn enough money to keep her son happy and healthy.

"No, sir!" Daryl's smile began to grow so large you could see each individual brace and the purple and gold bands on each of them.

"Did you walk?" And before he could answer, a tall black man in a military uniform came out around the corner with a smile bigger than Daryl's. "Jacob!" Mr. R shouted. And faster than any of us could move, Mr. R wheeled down the ramp onto the walkway right to the tall military man. "I can't believe you're home! How long have you been back? Are you home for good?" Mr. R was going rapid fire on the questions.

Jacob is Daryl's older brother. He jumped into the Marines right after he graduated high school. The guy has been stationed all around the world. And the only reason he did it was to help support his mom and brother after their dad died. His paycheck goes straight to his mom every month and she saves it. Recently Jacob has been stationed in Japan. He's so cool! Did you know you can still write letters and send them in the mail? Since he gets limited access to Skype and Facebook, Jacob writes everyone a letter in his spare time. I get my letters on Tuesdays. They always have long stories about the random adventures he goes on.

Like this one time, he wrote me a whole letter just about the vending machines in Japan. Another time he told me about how he met some local farmers while he was on his daily run and they told him stories of their adventures through Asia. How they climbed Mount Everest and even met the Dalai Lama. Jacob is like a real-life version of Dungeons and Dragons!

"I wish I was, Matt. I really do. But I'm only on leave for a couple more days. They gave me my two weeks off. That was about ten days ago," Jacob laughed after doing the math on his stay. "I've been working at the 7/11 with my mom to help her nab a few more bucks before I ship out to England, Tuesday." Looking at Jacob was like looking at a pro-athlete. His arms were jacked and he towered over us. He had to be like eight feet tall or something! "But just because I'm in town doesn't mean Daryl has to miss hanging out with you guys. You need your healer, don't you?" Jacob chuckled as he gave Daryl a little shove. "So, what's tonight's adventure got in store?"

"That's a secret. A good Dungeon Master never reveals his plans beforehand. Can't have these kiddos meta-gaming on me," Mr. R proclaimed, as he let out an ominous chuckle.

"Well then... I can't wait to hear about it later when I come back to pick Little Man up," Jacob said, giving Daryl's 'fro a tousle.

"Why don't you stay and play with us, Jake? That is if you're not too cool to play with a bunch of kids?" Liam offered. He gave Jacob a few quick punches to the stomach. Liam pulled back, shaking his hand as he did earlier.

"Maybe the question is whether you kids could keep up with your uncle and me?" Jacob laughed, as he took Liam in a head-lock and gave him a noogie. "But if y'all have room at the table for me, I'd love to stay if it's alright with the others," Jacob motioned toward Daryl and me.

"Hell yeah, you can play!" I shouted in excitement, and then looked around making sure nobody noticed me swear. And boy did they. Everybody was staring at me with that look. You know the one when a kid swears in front of you and you're not sure what to do. But nobody said anything. So I just went along with the silence.

"Daryl? What's your say?" Mr. R asked.

"I guess it's cool," Daryl answered reluctantly. "Couldn't say no to you, big bro. I mean how often will you be around to play? Here, you'll need these," Daryl said as he opened his bag and reached inside. He pulled out a black folder and a felt bag. The folder had Jacob written across the front of it in silver marker. Jacob reached out to grab the folder and felt pouch.

"Ah, Gimble my old friend, it has been too long," Jacob smiled at the folder. He then opened the little pouch and dumped the contents out into his hand. The seven different polyhedral dice were all sparkly and blue. He grabbed the twenty-sided die from the pile in his hand and raised it up in the air. "And boy did I miss you, my lucky little friend." He exclaimed as he moved the die to his lips and kissed it.

As Jacob moved to put away the dice, a car pulled up into the driveway. The Subaru hatchback parked next to Jacob's Sierra. Boy, did the car begin to look much smaller next to his truck. You could hear the music still blasting from the car. It was Bubble Dream by Chon. So that could mean only one thing. It was Ben! But more importantly, his sister, Laura.

What? No! I don't have a crush on her or anything! That's stupid! Why would anyone think that? It doesn't matter anyway. She's Ben's sister. That would be messed up. Whatever, I don't like her and that's it. She plays with us on Friday nights. I don't know why. She probably is just a more intelligent teenager who doesn't need to go to parties and get into trouble. Instead, she hangs with cool guys like me.

"Ahh, right on time! That's everyone. Why don't we go inside before it gets too dark." Mr. R turned around and headed back up the ramp and into the house. We all began to follow suit.

"I'll be right there, guys. I gotta get the rest of my dice from the truck! Jake, toss me your keys?" Daryl yelled as he started towards the black pickup in the driveway. Jacob pulled out his keys and tossed them right to Daryl, but he still missed them. He reached down to pick them up and ran to the truck. I went back inside behind Liam and headed for the kitchen. I moved straight to the fridge and grabbed a root beer.

"Careful there, Jack, remember what your mom said." Liam's uncle warned from the table in the next room. "I don't want her to stop bringing you because you're all hopped up on sugar. What would we do without our barbarian?"

"Oh, don't worry about that, Mr. R! She's been working that same Friday night bar shift since forever ago," I joked. "She would never stop me from coming. Might get too paranoid with me at home alone. Come up with some crazy crackpot theory that I'm gonna start doing drugs or something. She'd go insane."

"I believe you. Just take it easy, ok?"

"Yes, sir," I sighed.

"Hey, Jack, while you're in there, grab me one, too. I'm dying," Laura shouted out to me. Laura! Can you imagine that? Laura talked to me!

"Sure thing!" I shouted out. I reached back into the fridge and grabbed another soda. I made my way into the other room. As I walked in, I took in the amazing room. Mr. R had a passion for board games and role playing games. He had shelves full of games. Everything from Lanterns and Steam Park to Star Wars Rebellion and Empire Assault. But the pièce de résistance—the homemade game table. Mr. R had made this table back in high school with Jacob. They did it for their wood shop final their senior year. Which was like a billion years ago. But this relic had lasted and been upgraded. Before Jacob left for Japan, he and Mr. R added a flat screen TV in the table for computer use on a bigger level, for displaying maps and such during the games.

They even added wiring and outlets for charging phones and tablets.

"Ok, I'm back, guys." It was Daryl coming back into the house. He walked into the room and dropped his huge case thing on the table with a loud thud. The contents inside shifted around. It was one of those sewing boxes quilters use to keep their thread organized. But Daryl didn't bring thread. When he opened the lid, it exposed to us what he was hiding. The box had every set of dice Daryl owned. All organized by color and die. The case was seven by ten. And each compartment had dice in them. Each row a different die, each column a different color. "I finally was able to organize all my dice. Anyone else impressed?" Daryl had a huge smirk of pride. "Now the real question is... which ones are the lucky dice?" Daryl took the next twenty minutes to roll each twenty-sided die multiple times until he found the "luckiest" five he had. "Okay, guys... I think I'm ready." And right as Daryl made his proclamation, Mr. R's phone went off saying there was motion at the front door.

"Jack, Liam, will you two go grab that?" Mr. R asked us. I made my way to the front door, unlocked it, and swung it wide open. And there on the porch stood the man of the hour.

"Wade! My man! How goes the pizza runs tonight?" I asked. Wade is the guy who always ends up delivering our pizzas on Friday.

"What's going on, my dudes? I got a special delivery for ya." Wade smiled at us as he pulled out the pizzas from the insulated bag thing. "I've got five pizzas here. Two cheese, one pepperoni, a sausage, and of course the Jack special; sausage, green pepper, and mushroom." Wade handed the pizzas to Liam who then took them into the kitchen. I reached into my pocket and pulled out ten bucks from the wad of cash my mom left for pizza. Or babysitting. Either way, it's getting used.

"Here, Wade, for your troubles," I said as I casually slipped the ten bucks into his hand through a handshake.

"Whoa-ho! That was slick, little dude. Where'd you learn that?" Wade said, looking at the ten bucks in his hand.

"I've been watching Friends on Netflix recently. Picked up on some tricks." Besides watching Twitch streams of Critical Role, Mom and I had been watching older shows on Netflix.

"What a killer trick my dude. Just for that, I've got a little treat for you guys. Kurtis told me to give it to you dudes." Wade reached into the bag again and pulled out another pizza box. But this box was about half the size of the others. I opened it up to see what was inside. And lo and behold, it was a cookie and brownie pizza. We call it a Kurtis special. It's a cookie, baked with brownie mix in the cookie dough. They send it with Wade every once in awhile as a kind of like a customer reward thing, ya know?

"Thanks, Wade. Tell K-man we appreciate it, like always."

"Anytime, little dude! Role me some criticals tonight, a'ight?" Wade said as he began walking down the ramp.

"You know it, man. Keep it real." As I said this Wade threw his fist into the air with his pinky and thumb extended.

"Righteous! I'll catch y'all next week. Until then, my dude!" Wade said as he began to get into his car.

I took the Kurtis special to the kitchen and set it next to the already open pizzas. I grabbed myself a plate from the stack next to the pizzas and opened up my box. I picked a few of the peppers off and popped them in my mouth before I sat down at my spot at the table. As I went to sit in my chair, I realized I never took off my bag. This heavy sack had been on my back since I walked in almost an hour and a half ago. I never even noticed it. I slipped off the bag and felt the release of the literal weight off my shoulders. I reached into my bag and pulled out my binder with all my notes and character sheets inside. I pulled out my large dice bag, set it on the table, opened the top up and rifled through until I found my lucky set. Glossy pink with sparkles on them and a black and red metal d20. (In case you're new to my world, all dice are referred to as d and then the number of sides it has. So a twenty-sided die is called a d20) I lined my dice up from smallest to largest, each with the highest number facing up. Gotta run with my superstitions even if they don't work a thousand percent of the time. It's part of the fun of playing D&D.

"Alright, you guys. Who is ready to jump back into the adventure?" Liam's uncle proclaimed in his booming announcer voice.

"AYE!" I shout with a deep graveled voice with an undertone of a Scottish accent, thus transforming myself into Adrik Frostbeard!

2

MEET THE PARTY

"Okay, let's get a recap of last week," Mr. R said as he wheeled up to his side of the table. He pulled his dice pouch from his lap and placed it in front of himself. He then proceeded to take his laptop from the bag that hung from the back of his chair, plugging in the HDMI cable in the flat screen TV in the center of the table. It lit up with a chime, and his computer interface appeared in the center of the table. He began to pull out his Dungeon Master screen, unfolding the four flaps, hiding his dice and notes from our view.

"So, last time we left off, our heroes were deep in the in the Dark Forest after being sent on a quest to find the Temple of the Raven Queen. Your party traversed through the quicksand pits, avoided the Hag of the Forest, and then set up camp. You all fell asleep and got ambushed in the night by a pack of goblins. To your luck, the heroes managed to survive the attack. We now find our adventurers tearing down their camp and smothering the fire. Any questions before we start?" Mr. R paused and looked at each person.

"Can we restore our hit points since we rested after that

attack?" Ben asked raising his pencil in the air to show he had a question. Ben is always a stickler about being at full health.

"Ahhh, good catch," Mr. R responded nodding at Ben. "Everyone can restore their characters to full health, and you gain all those spell slots back. Thank you, Ben." Each person took their pencils and started erasing on their character sheets. I felt relieved to erase that ninety-five on my sheet and return to a hundred and five. I even regained all my rages. Those are too useful not to have. "Anyone else?" Mr. R asked one more time. "Alright then. If everyone could close their eyes," Mr. R instructed. One by one we all closed our eyes. Some of us even bowed our heads. "Let's start to my left, Ront. Are you here with us?"

"Hmph!" Liam responded to his uncle.

"Adrik, my friend, are you here?" Mr. R asked.

"Aye," I called out with my graveled Scottish accent. Mimicking the dwarven trait the best I could.

"Good, good. How about you, Rolen? Have you come to join us?" Mr. R asked.

"I am here. With the will of nature to help guide us," Ben called out to the group. I opened my right eye just a little to see Ben standing and aiming his imaginary staff to the center of the group.

"Glad to hear it my friend. Torinn, how goes it?" Mr. R asked. I caught a glimpse of his large smile before I closed my eyes again.

"Ahh, yes my friend, it goes well. My shield is yours to use. May the good Lord Pelor bless our journey on this beautiful afternoon!" Daryl called out. His Ian McKellen impersonation was almost spot on. Sometimes you forget that these are just characters. Especially Daryl and Torinn. They are two different people but in one person. Ya know what I mean?

"May they bestow safe passage to you and your friends.

Lerissa, my darling, have you graced us with your presence tonight?" Mr. R asked.

"Ahhh, yes. I am here, my friends. I bring the knowledge of the elements to our aid, in hopes that we shall find our path!" Laura exclaimed in her enchanting voice. So, strong and powerful, yet sweet to the ear. I peeked out again to see her actions in response to the DM.

She had her eyes wide open and was giving a grand gesture with her arms spread out. Our eyes met and locked on to each other. She had a large, gorgeous smile that went cheek to cheek, exposing her dimples. Those beautiful dimples. I began to get hot in my face. Was I blushing? What, no! Why would I be? Am I smiling too? Oh man, she sees it too! As I begin to panic about my involuntary facial expressions, Laura shot me a quick wink. Oh man. My heart started pounding against my chest faster and faster. Am I having a heart attack? Does anyone else smell burnt toast?

"Happy to hear it, my dear. And let's not forget our good friend, Gimble! Are you with the party tonight, old friend?"

"Oh, you know it. May my talents and violin aid the party to victory. And of course, lead us to a tavern at the end full of ladies —and men!" Jacob called out with a roar. I still had my eyes open and caught Jacob nudge Laura with his elbow when he said men. I don't know why, but that made me a little angry. Not like I wanted to get up and punch Jake, because, I mean, I couldn't anyway. He'd demolish me. But it gave me that gut feeling. Like a stone in my stomach. I was upset, but I couldn't tell you why.

"Can't wait to hear what you come up with tonight," Mr. R responded. "It sounds like everyone is present. You all can open your eyes once you are fully ready." One by one we opened our eyes. I was the first open since I never closed them after watching Laura. She was the next to open her eyes. And again, we made eye contact. Next was Jacob, followed by Liam and Ben. But Daryl kept his eyes closed. They were closed so tight you could see the vein in his neck protruding. He was holding his breath. He began to turn red like the d20 in front of him. I was about to reach out and tap him to make sure he was ok, but then he started taking deep breaths. I knew he did deep breaths to get into character, but I've never seen him hold his breath first. The kid is dedicated though.

"Okay, you guys. You've all just taken down your camp in the middle of the forest. Lerissa, you are smothering the fire. You all take a few moments to gather and pack your things. Who wants to start?" Mr. R asked the group.

"I would like to kneel in the bit of sunlight breaking through the canopy with my holy symbol in front of me and pray," Daryl responded in his character, Torinn's voice. "Before we get too far and I forget."

"Do you mind if I join you? It has been quite some time since I sat and meditated with nature," Ben said to Daryl. Ben uses a slight English accent when in character, It's light, but it really does change him from Ben to Rolen the half-elf.

Torinn began to cough and mumble a little before responding, "By all means, my good friend. The more, the merrier," he responded. "I take a knee and place my holy symbol in front of myself."

"I lay my staff across my lap and sit facing Torinn," Ben directed.

"While you two are praying," Mr. R led, "What you are going to say?"

"To the Lord of Light, our giver of life. We reach out to you our lord and savior Pelor. We ask that you bless our adventure and travels with safety and wisdom. And may you find it in your heart to grant us the strength to save those who stand in our way. We thank you our Lord. May the Light guide us." Torinn prayed aloud. Both their heads were bowed, and Daryl had moved his arm to reach out to Ben's shoulder.

"When you two are finished talking to the air, will you please come and help me pack up the rations?" Liam hollered at the two, "We haven't got all day! We need to make it to the Temple in three days, or we miss our chance to retrieve the secret item the guy wanted!" Liam's voice for Ront was deep and menacing. Not quite as good as James Earl Jones, but he definitely had the same effect.

"Pelor isn't going to like that, my friend," Rolen responded to the half-orc.

"Well by how my life has been, it won't be the first or last time," Ront snickered.

"While these losers are arguing about whatever, I'm over sitting on a fallen tree sharpening my axe," I said. I began making the motion in the air. Moving my right arm in a downward motion, imagining a real axe being sharpened. "I'm ready to get a move on," I called out in my dwarvish voice. "Can y'all start moving? I've got a feeling there are more things out in this forest, and I'm ready to give them a smash and a split!"

"Lerissa is gonna move over next to Adrik and stand over him resting her chin on his head," Laura narrated. "Adrik, what's the rush? We still have a couple of days before we can even get into the Temple. Relax, enjoy the forest around you. Embrace your surroundings," Lerissa said to me. I felt a little tingle in my chest when she told me to relax.

"Adrik, will you give me a quick perception check?" Mr. R asked me.

"That's never good when the DM asks that out of the blue," I replied. I grabbed my pink d20 from the line up in front of me. I shook it around in my fisted hand before dropping it into the rubber surface of the table. It rolled out and across the table at Jacob.

"That's a twelve, my friend," Jake said, as he handed me back my die with the twelve facing out to show me the roll.

"Well, then it's a twelve on perception. My wisdom modifier is zero," I shifted my binder to show Mr. R my wisdom stat.

"Ok." He nodded. "Adrik, as Lerissa finishes telling you to relax and embrace your surroundings, you notice that the sky is beginning to become gloomy and cloudy. Like it might be about to rain," he explained. "Then suddenly," he paused. A bright flash on the TV screen in the table followed by a boom a couple of seconds later erupted. "You all can hear what sounds like distant rain slowly getting closer to the camp site."

"Oh, could this get any better?" Ront complained, "What happened to the high and mighty Pelor giving us safe passage?" he shouted at Torinn. "Where's your god now?"

"Oh, calm down, you non-believer," Torinn reassured him. "You never know, this could've been the Lord's doing! For all we know there was something in our way that hates rain. And now our path is cleared," he explained.

"You had better be right," Ront threatened. Ront is known to be a bit impatient. And definitely anti-religion. But it's not his fault he's like that. When he was younger, Ront grew up the son of an orc chief. His father demanded instant results from his son. But Ront wasn't what his father had expected. So, when he was still only a child, his father left him in the woods alone. Ront quickly had to adapt to the world. He began stealing to keep alive. Never having anyone but himself to rely on. Real sob story. But it's what makes Ront, Ront.

"Come on, let's get going. That storm isn't going to wait for us to get moving," I announced. "I start walking down the trail."

"Come on boys. We don't wanna lose the dwarf now. He may not even notice that we fell behind," Lerissa called out with a laugh. "Wouldn't be the first time he ditched us for something silly." Everyone chuckled simultaneously. Even Gimble.

"So? Do you all follow Adrik deeper into the woods?" Mr. R questioned the group.

"Follow the fool before he gets us killed, this forest is not very forgiving," Rolen called out. "For all we know there's another band of beasts ready to kill us. Rolen pulls himself off the ground and begins to follow Adrik."

"Alright then," Mr. R reacted. "You all set off onto the path. Adrik, taking the lead?" He questioned, raising his eyebrow.

"Yeah, but with me beside him so we don't get lost again," Laura replied. She shot me a smile and another wink. I almost fell off my chair!

"I-I won't get us lost—again," I groaned. I knew it would happen, but no way Adrik admit would that. It's one of his traits on my character sheet. *Adrik never admits defeat, not even at death.*

"Sure, whatever you say." She winked at me for the third time! What is she doing? Is she a real wizard? Trying to trance me? I can't succumb to her evil powers! Not tonight!

"Alright. Adrik and Lerissa lead the group down the path further into the Dark Forest. The longer you all walk, the more the light disappears. After a bit of travel, the forest is as dark as night," Mr. R described. "With each of your characters having dark-vision, you can still see each other. But slowly it begins to close in on the group. Your circle of vision grows smaller and smaller until—you can't see your own hand in front of your face!" Mr. R was waving his hands all mystically as if he were really casting some sort of spell or whatnot.

"I want to cast dispel magic," Laura announced to us.

"Ah, would you now?" Mr. R asked her, raising the other eyebrow this time.

"Yeah. If it's magic causing this darkness we have to get rid of it to see," she responded with a bit of condescension. I mean she isn't wrong. We need to see. But when the DM questions you, it's usually not a good thing.

"And how would you go about casting that spell?" he questioned. There was a tinge of sarcasm in his voice as he raised his eyebrow again.

"I'm going to read the spell out of my spell book to cast it," Laura responded snarkily.

"Okay," Mr. R replied, with a bit of a pique in his voice followed by a chuckle. "I'm going to tell you now it won't work." He smiled at her with a menacing smile.

"What do you mean it's not gonna work?" Laura shouted out, leaping from her chair. She threw her hand into her bag and ripped out her player's handbook. She began searching through the spell list in the back. "Dispel... Dispel.... Where is it?" She stopped suddenly and looked up at everyone. "I'm dumb, aren't I? I can't cast anything here as a wizard, huh? Since it's too frickin' dark to read my damn book!" She shouted as she slapped her hand into her book.

"There, she got it!" Mr. R cried out. "I wanted to see how long this was going take for you to realize that. I was thinking you were going read the entire handbook before you picked up on what happened." He laughed out. "Anyone else have a plan then?"

Daryl lifted his head after laughing at Laura for so long. "I'll cast dispel magic," he announced, shooting Laura a thumbs-up and a cheesy smile.

"Okay then. Suddenly you all hear Torinn speak out into the darkness and cast his spell. Your vision begins to come back. Starting from a small pinhole and gradually growing larger and larger until you have full vision again. You observe the area around you and notice that you're not where you last remember. The path is nowhere to be seen, and the trees are close and dense around you. Trees that stand ten to twenty feet high tower over and crowd you all. What do you guys do?" Mr. R asked. He reminds me of a hippy that you see on TV when he describes the landscape. He always has his hands waving and flowing in front of him. Like he's trying to mimic the wind and the trees blowing around.

"I want to climb a tree and go see the surrounding area," Ben called out.

"What's your dexterity?" Mr. R responds.

"Eleven," Ben said, a smirk curling on the side of his mouth.

"Alright, you climb up the tree with some difficulty, but you make it. Roll me a perception check now since you're looking around the area up top."

Ben reached out for the d20 in front of him, gave it a little stir in his fist and gently laid it on the table. "Erm..." Ben grumbled staring at his roll. "That's a seven total."

"Okay. As you break through the thick canopy of the forest, daylight hits your eyes with a burning light. Your eyes are hurting to adjust. You look in every direction but see nothing more than trees for the little bit you can see, being partially blinded by the sun," Mr. R explained to the poor half-elf. Ben's face dropped, but still had that slight smirk on it.

"Can I cast plant growth and cover myself from the light?" Ben asked, as he picked up his d20 again.

"Why not? After coming up to the bright sunlight and being temporarily blinded, you cast plant growth, and through your arcane ability, you feel the branches from the trees beneath you begin to grow and create a little umbrella above you, shielding you from the sunlight. Go ahead and reroll your perception," Mr. R instructed. Again, he moves his arms and fingers as if he were the tree branches magically growing.

Ben shook his fist again. This time he wasn't gentle on the roll. He let that thing ricochet off each wall of the table, bouncing like a pinball. Miraculously the die landed right in front of him. He looked up at us. "Well, that should do it. I rolled a sixteen. Add my five wisdom modifier, making it a twenty-one total!" Ben calculated out loud. That cheesy smirk grew into a huge smile. His invisible braces peering out from behind his lips.

"Alrighty then," Mr. R said with a hint of shock in his voice. "After your eyes adjust to the new light you begin to see smoke in the distance. Nothing huge like a wildfire. But enough smoke to catch your attention. The thick black smoke trails into the sky for a while before it fades into the clouds." Mr. R looked to the ceiling, mimicking the smoke trail with his arms.

"Oh boy, that's gonna be fun! I'm gonna climb back down and tell the group," Ben exclaimed. "I slide down the tree and began explaining to the party. Ok, there is smoke coming up from that direction." He pointed out randomly. "If there's smoke then that means there is somebody there. Maybe even a tavern or shops. I think we should go that direction."

"I don't know," Torinn muttered. "What if that smoke isn't a good sign? What if that's the rest of that goblin horde, that are camping out further up the trail? This could be an ambush," he said. It's always a good idea to have a pessimist in the group. If it wasn't for Daryl and his fear of losing Torinn, we wouldn't have made it past level five. He has saved us many a time just by being scared to fully jump in. It is annoying at times, but it comes in handy other times.

"You're always paranoid, Tor," I responded. "Sometimes you just gotta go all in. We've already shown that we can take them if they're goblins. What's to be afraid of?" I asked as I gave Torinn a friendly punch in the shoulder.

"Yes, I'm paranoid. You would be too if you had almost died against the first group," Daryl snapped back. "I have almost exactly half your health, and I took four times the amount of damage in that last fight. I'm not willing to almost die two times in a row."

Daryl was standing out of his chair now. His face was slightly red, and you could see that he was a bit upset about the idea of going into another round of combat.

"Okay, okay. Everyone calm down," Ront interjected. Liam stretched his hand to Daryl's shoulder. Daryl sat back down. He moved his hand up behind his ear and adjusted his hearing aids. He then took his open hand and tapped his thumb on his chest to sign *I'm fine*.

"Okay, everyone take a breath," Ront instructed. "We're going to be okay. Let's go towards the smoke..." He stopped to put his hand up to Torinn before he could interrupt him. "And we will go quietly and carefully as to not provoke an attack. We will scout it out and see if it's going to be a safe place to go. If not we will try to sneak around the danger and continue out of the forest. Does that sound like a plan?" He stopped and looked around at everyone.

"I can live with that plan. I don't like the idea of getting close to another group of goblins, but I guess we have no choice at this point." Torinn sighed.

"I'll keep you safe my friend, don't you worry," I assured Torinn. I stretched my arm out to him. He reached out and clasped his hand around my forearm. He always panics about the what if's, but I'll always be there to protect my friends in the face of danger.

"Well then let's get moving," Lerissa instructed. "We need to hurry to our destination. We have a small window of time, and we're wasting it by arguing. Rolen, you know where the smoke is at, you're taking the lead," Laura exclaimed as she pointed at her brother.

"Alright let's get a move on," Rolen exclaimed.

Mr. R asked the party as he clicked his spacebar on his laptop. "You all set off down the trail again. The little bit of dirt trail that remains under the overgrown forest is just enough to guide you out. You walk for a couple of hours, and finally, you reach the end of the forest. Almost as if an invisible wall was made here, the tree line just stops abruptly. From there you can see a paved road that stretches for miles through the flat plains before you. And out in the distance, you can see the rising smoke on the horizon. What do you all do?" There on the screen in the table was an image of the land he described to us. The grass stretched across miles of open land. Little hills roll across the screen. Just as depicted.

"There it is you guys. The smoke. Let's go. There's probably a town or something there that we could settle at," Rolen called out "And I run down the road towards the smoke."

"While you start running forward, give me a perception check real quick, Ben," Mr. R said. You could see him holding back a massive smile as to not give away any surprises. But he's never been good at hiding his facial expressions.

"No! Don't do this to me! I just saved us!" Ben cried out as he hesitantly scooped up his die. He rolled it in his fist for what felt like forever. Making a shamed face at Liam's uncle, probably trying to get him not to make him roll. But Mr. R just sat there and smiled at him. "Ugh," Ben grunted. "Why is it always me? This is what I get for trying to take point?" He finally let go of his d20. We sit and watch in anticipation. en. Fourteen. Five... One. "Oh, you have to be freaking kidding me!" A smile that stretched from ear to ear came across Mr. R's face.

"As Rolen begins down the road, running towards the smoke, you all watch as he trips over what appears to be nothing. As he slides across the dirt pavement, he suddenly disappears from view," Mr. R explained.

"I'm going to carefully go up and see what happened. Can I percept for traps?" Ront responded.

"No, as you get closer, Ront, you see that there was a trip wire that is now pulled from its position across the road and is now staked on one side while the other stake is missing. You walk further up the path and see a hole in the ground. The trip wire leads down the hole. As you finally get close enough to look in the hole you see Rolen curled in a ball of pain on the ground," Mr. R described. "Rolen, you take..." He starts rolling dice behind his screen. "10 falling damage."

"Crap!" Rolen blurted out. "I'm okay! Little scraped up, but nothing Torinn can't fix. Can someone help me out? Maybe toss some rope down?"

"I'll help you out of the pit on one condition," Ront shouted down into the hole. "I'll throw you down some rope if you admit you're an idiot and should let the rogue take the lead next time to check for traps."

"Ugh, do I have to?" Rolen groaned. "Mmmmm, fine! I'm an idiot, and I should let you take the lead next time to check for traps. There. Happy?" Rolen muttered at Ront.

"Better," Ront chuckled. "I pull out a long spool of rope from my pack and toss one end down the hole. Then I tie the other end around my waist," Liam narrated. "Will someone come hold me back before this idiot pulls me down there with him?" he shouted out to the party.

"Aye, I'll hold ya," I responded. "Adrik is gonna take his axe out and bury the blade into the ground behind him before reaching for the rope around Ront's waist," I said. "Ready!" I nodded to Liam.

"Okay. Both of you give me strength checks with advantage." Mr. R said to Liam, Ben, and me. We each grabbed our d20s and shook them in our fists. One by one we each let go of our die. Ten, Fifteen, Eight. We grab again and reroll our advantage. This time like clockwork we roll simultaneously. Eighteen, another Fifteen, and a Two.

"Do-da-do," Liam sang out followed by a couple of tongue clicks. His finger traced around his character sheet until it found what he was looking for. "Eighteen plus three makes it a twenty-one!"

"I've got fifteen plus four giving me a nineteen," I said with a huge smile on my face.

"Well poop!" Ben blurted. "Eight plus two make a ten," His voice getting higher as he winces at the ten.

"Okay. So Ront pulls on the rope with all his half-orc strength," Mr. R began. "Adrik holds tight onto both Ront's rope belt and his axe in the dirt. Both grunting. Muscles rippling. Rolen trying his hardest to climb the rope. Making some effort but not as much as the combined strength of his friends on the surface. It takes a couple of minutes, but Rolen finally reaches the top of the hole and begins to scurry up and out of it."

"Rolen rolls out of the pit and lays there on the ground panting for air. Ah, thanks, mates, I owe ya one," Rolen said between breaths. "So how about that smoke?"

"Well if you're done fooling around, I'd like to get a move on," Lerissa said.

"Torinn is clanking behind her in his armor," Daryl described.

"I reach down to Rolen and lift him up out of the dirt and onto his feet," Lerissa said. "This time I'm on lead with Tor, okay?"

"But Ront said..." Rolen started before Lerissa interrupted.

"I don't care what he said," she commanded. "I'm going to lead because you lot are going to get us killed. If I need it, Ront will check for traps. But we need to survive to find out what this damn smoke is, and whether it's going to get us killed or help us out."

"Okay then, your highness." Rolen bowed. "Behind you we go." Ben rolled his eyes at his sister as siblings do. When I glanced over to see what her reaction was, Laura was already looking back down at her papers. She glanced up without moving her head, pencil end between her teeth. Her eyes locked onto mine—and she winked at me again! I could feel the blood rush around my body. Away from my brain and into my cheeks. My heart was pounding again, probably trying to pump all this blood that isn't where it should be. Why am I all flustered? She's Ben's sister! That's so gross!

"Jack, you okay?" Mr. R's voice broke through my train of thought.

"W-what?" I sputtered out. "Oh y-yeah, I'm good! Just got lost in thought for a sec. All good." I threw up both my fists, protruding my thumbs high into the air.

"Alright, you guys head up the road again towards the smoke..." Mr. R paused. He began looking at his laptop and scrolling his fingers across the trackpad. "As you begin to come over the top of the small hill, you all see a town about a mile out. The smoke coming from the middle area. As you get closer, you all notice the layout of the town. Most homes and shops look like they're more centralized in the town while the few farm homes and plots are on the outskirts or in the distance away from everyone else. You can see a couple of carts being drawn by horses, passing between the buildings. The sound of children's laughter fills the air as you watch as group of children chase what looks to be like a ball. The road you all are on leads right into the center of town. Do you go in?"

3

NEED A SHORT REST?

"I'm going in!" I shouted to the group. "There has to be a shop or tavern in here. And this dwarf needs a pint!" I exclaimed pointing a thumb at my chest. "Adrik lifts one leg in the air, spins around on the other foot and begins walking to the town."

"Guess we're going in?" Rolen questioned the others. "I don't see the harm in a thirsty dwarf. Maybe we can pick up some potions or something while we're here."

"Fine," Lerissa and Ront moaned in unison.

"But tomorrow we have to hoof it," Lerissa scolded. "We're running out of time. And I'd rather not pay the consequence of that contract you guys signed. I still don't trust the guy."

"Hey, Uncle Matt, what's the time looking like?" Liam asked.

"You guys did spend quite some time walking. Let's say it's later in the afternoon," Mr. R calculated. "It's still light out, but you can see that the sun is on its way behind the God's Peak Mountains."

"Let's just rest up in this town then. Regain anything we're missing." Ront glared at Rolen. "Then we can set off in the morning and hopefully make it in time."

"Whatever," Laura rolled her eyes. "It's your funerals if that guy turned out to be a devil or something. And I'm gonna sit here laughing at all of you when you're rerolling characters." She scowled as she finally opened the can of root beer I had given her.

"We're fine, don't sweat it." Liam chuckled.

"Ok, you guys begin back down the road," Mr. R began. "You reach the town center and take a look around. The town isn't crazy busy. But for a small town, this is probably what it looks like at its busiest. Most street vendors are packing up their carts and horses for the night. There's one cart in particular that catches your eye. There are two men. One goliath and one gnome. The goliath is wheeling a small cart while the gnome rides holding a torch in his hand. As they get closer, you notice that they are lighting all the street lamps and torches around. The sun is now almost gone behind the mountains, but you notice that the light never faded."

Mr. R changed his facial expression. He scrunched his eyebrows, and he pushed his jaw out to make it look more square. "Is that all of them?" He grunted in a low, gravelly voice.

Then all of a sudden his face changed again. This time it was bright and cheery. His eyebrows up high on his forehead and a huge smile stretched across his face. "We sure are! I say it's high time for us to go get a drink!" Mr. R responded to himself. "What do ya say? The Dragon's Tale then?"

"Whatever, so long as it's your turn to pay!" The goliath said to the gnome.

"You guys watch as the goliath wheels the cart into the alley-way, scoops up the gnome and plops him on his shoulder. Then they take off down the road," Mr. R described, changing back to his regular voice and face. "So, what do you all wanna do? The sun is now set, and almost all the people walking in town seem to be heading in one direction."

"I heard drinks at the Dragon's Tale," I chimed. "That's where I'm off to! Adrik takes off down the road following the goliath and gnome."

"I'm gonna follow him," Rolen said. "Make sure he doesn't get in any trouble. I'd rather not be chased out of another town because he woke up a tarrasque again. And Rolen begins jogging down the road after the dwarf."

"Well," Torinn began before coughing. "I want to find a shop that would be open at this hour. Hopefully, one who sells healing potions and such. Would you like to join me, my dear?" Torinn asked as he extended his arm out for Lerissa to take.

"Better than watching those two get wasted," Lerissa chuckled. "What are you going to be up to then, Ront?"

"I'm going to keep my eye on Tweedledee and Tweedledum," Ront responded. "But I'm keeping my distance and out of sight just as a precaution. You guys be careful," Liam said. "Ront makes his way down the road where both Adrik and Rolen went."

"Awesome. Can I get perception checks from all of you?" Mr. R asked. Everyone picked up and dropped their dice.

"I've got a six," I responded.

"Eleven," Liam announced.

"Fourteen," Daryl said.

"I rolled a three, but it's a total of eight after modifiers" Ben sighed.

"Thirteen," Laura said.

"Okay, Ront," Mr. R began. "You quickly are able to find the other two amongst the thin crowd making their way down the road. Roll me a stealth check real quick."

Liam rolled his die and looked up to his uncle with a toothy grin. "I rolled an eighteen," he started. "But my stealth is plus thirteen, so it's a thirty-one total. I'm so stealthy I can't even see myself."

"Well then..." Mr. R shook his head and laughed. "Nobody even notices you as you stand just feet behind them. As for my two out on a mission for potions. It takes you guys a bit of time. Long enough for Torinn to bore you a little with one of his lengthy stories you have probably heard many times before." Mr. R chuckled.

"Have I ever told you about the time that I single-handedly slew a dragon that was attacking my temple?" Torinn begins telling Lerissa. "Many ages back when I was much, much younger, you see. An ancient white dragon came to my home temple in Dracomear. Why he attacked my village is beyond any of us. Maybe he wasn't happy about dragonborns worshiping Pelor instead of Tiamat. Thanks to my faith in the good Lord Pelor I was given the power to defeat the nasty beast. But not before obtaining a few scars you see." Daryl ran his open hand across his face where Torinn's snout would be to emphasize the massive scars from his battle. "But I persisted, and look at me now. Seventy years young and still fighting the good fight with my friends!"

"Ahh, good to hear that story again, Tor," Lerissa responded sarcastically.

Fighting through laughter, Mr. R started again, "You both find a shop that still has a light on inside."

"I drop Torinn's arm and go inside," Laura explained.

"Well then, I guess I follow!" Daryl called out.

"You both walk into the store. As you open the door, you hear the bell ring that indicated someone had walked in. You begin hearing things falling over and crashing in the back, followed by what sounds like indescribable cursing." Mr. R said as he began setting the scene. The TV in the table changed again. This time showing an image of a cluttered little shop.

"Hello?" Lerissa called out into the shop. "Is there anyone here?"

"Coming!" Mr. R responded. "The voice is coming from the back room behind the counter, across the room from both of you."

"We're looking to purchase some wares if you have what we need," Lerissa called out again. As she spoke, a little gnome image appeared on the screen behind the counter in the art.

"Ah yes, what can I do for ya, my dear?" Mr. R said. His voice was slightly higher than his regular voice, and he had a bit of an Irish accent.

"Yes, hello good friend," Torinn spoke up. "We were looking to see if you had any potions or items of magic in this shop. Possibly a potion of healing?"

"Ahh, I see," Mr. R responded. "Well let's have a look, shall we? And he ducks under the counter. When he comes back up, he sets a case down on the counter with a thud and clink of glass," he described. "Let's take a look in here. He pops open the case and inside are dozens of vials and bottles full of different colored liquids. He begins rifling through them all. "Let's see—flying—no, no, no that won't do," he said to himself. "We have a potion for climbing," he said. He holds up a bottle filled with brown, silver, and gray layers of liquid. "And this one is firebreath." This one has an orange liquid that flickers. The top of the bottle is filled with smoke. "And oh, here is that invisibility potion I've been looking for." He rotates the bottle in his hand, and the liquid inside floats to the top of the bottle. "Ah, here we are!" He paused. "The gnome holds up a bottle of red liquid that glimmers as he shakes it. I believe these are what you're searching for? The gnome pulled out more bottles resembling it. He lines up all the bottles in a row on the counter."

"Are they all the same potency?" Torinn asked. "You know, some regular, some greater?"

"Oh, I have them all my friend," Mr. R said joyously. "All

potencies. Normal, greater, superior, and one or two supreme. Do any of these interest you?"

"Oh my, they do, my good friend." Torinn chuckled. "What is your price of these fine potions?"

"Let's see." The gnome rummages under the counter before pulling up a small sheet of parchment. "For the regular, one gold piece. And the supreme is one hundred gold pieces."

"Oh my. Well, let me talk to my young friend here real quick." Torinn motioned to Lerissa. "How many can we get?" he whispered.

"Well, Tor, we can get a couple. Unless you want to get the supreme ones," Lerissa said. "I'm not about to let you spend all of our money on potions. We still need a place to stay for the night. And you sure as hell know that we are going to cover the damages and tabs of the others when we catch up to them."

"Oh, alright," Torinn responded. "Can I get one supreme and a few greater? Just a couple?" he begged.

"Fine," Lerissa responded. "Here is a hundred and fifty gold." Laura mimed handing Daryl a small pouch.

"There we are," Torinn said as he turned back to Mr. R. "My good friend, let me get one supreme and two greater potions please!"

"Ah, sure thing, my good friend," Mr. R said. "He hands Torinn the three red potions requested."

"Torinn hands the pouch of gold to the gnome and collects his potions.

"Is there anything else you might be looking to gather? Any oddities or peculiar items?" Mr. R asked in his gnome voice.

"I wish I could, but my lovely friend over here only gave me enough for the potions," Torinn told the gnome. "But maybe tomorrow if we have the funds," he whispered with a wink.

"Then I will see you all next time." Mr. R smiled. "He scurries out from behind the counter and escorts you both out the door. Once you two are out the door, it slams behind you both, and you can hear locks clicking and sliding." Mr. R described. "And then the lights go out in the windows. What do you guys do?"

"I guess we go meet the others at the tavern?" Torinn asked Lerissa.

"Let's see what trouble they're already in," Lerissa joked.

"Alrighty then," Mr. R chuckled. "Looks like it's up to you now, boys. So, what're you up to after finding the tavern by following the town people to it?"

"Well, wasn't it obvious?" Adrik called out of my mouth. "We are drinkin' and gettin' to know the locals."

"I'm making sure Tweedledum here doesn't get into any trouble that almost kills us again." Rolen paused. "But I'm drinking with the little man here." He laughed as he nudged my shoulder.

"Well, boys, what're ya havin' tonight?" Mr. R asked. This time his eyebrow was raised, elbow on the table. His voice was welcoming with a little scratch to it.

"Aye what you got that'll get this well-seasoned dwarf loose and drunk?" I asked slamming my fist on the table.

"Ahh, give the young lad-" Mr. R said before he mimicked a hiccup. "Give 'em the good ole' mead that I've been drinkin' for years!" Mr. R said acting as if he were drunk. "Sorry, my friends." The bartender came back. "That there is Benji. War hero to some. Local drunk to all. The man practically lives here. I take good care of ole' Benji."

"Aye-" Benji interjected followed with a hiccup. "I 'ave been here for many years ya see—" He hiccupped again. "Benji is a stout dwarf. Unlike Adrik he wears no armor." Mr. R described. "After the wars that I fought in for almost two centuries—" another hiccup. "I started wandering the world. A couple decades ago I—" and another hiccup. "I landed here in Faria, at this here pub." Benji slapped the bar.

"Well then!" I shouted. "I'm having what Benji is having! If it can make a dwarf like him stay for this long, it has to be good."

"Comin' right up, my friend," Mr. R's bartender responded. "And, uh, something for you?" He pointed at Ben.

"Well," Rolen pondered. "What ya got?" Mr. R looked at Ben and gave him a laugh.

"We have a bottle of anything you could imagine. He turns around and points at the vast wall behind him. Kegs and bottles stretch the entire wall." Mr. R explained as he hit his keyboard. And there on the screen was an image of the Dragon's Tale. "I've got things from across the world, things from other planes of existence, and the even some from the gods themselves."

"Very impressive, I must say," Rolen said trying to hide his surprise. "Well, what do you have from my home, Xiloscent?"

"Ahhh, my pointy eared friend," Mr. R smiled, "This fine bottle here. And he reaches to the highest shelf and pulls down a dusty black bottle. A red ribbon tied around the neck and a red wax seal to bring it all together," Mr. R explained. "How does this sound? It predates your empire. Back before Xiloscent began claiming land, not that long ago. This, my friend, is a bottle of shimmer water. That tickle your fancy?" he asked "He pulls out two glasses and sets them on the bar."

"Give it to me," Rolen exclaimed in excitement. "I grab the glass and down my drink." Ben winced and shook his head before choking a little and then finally coughing a bit, like he drank something really strong. "That—" He choked a bit more. "That is much stronger than the shimmer water I remember!"

"That's because you probably get that watered-down crap they make now." Mr. R laughed as he mimed pouring Rolen another glass. "He pours some liquid into a mug and hands it to

Adrik," he explained. "Bottoms up, my new frien'!" he said as Benji to me, and he began mimicking chugging his drink.

"Cheers to that, ya crazy!" I shouted and followed suit.

"Alrighty, I need constitution checks from both of you," Mr. R told us. We grabbed our dice and gave them a roll.

"That's a nice eight." Ben laughed.

"Sixteen," I announced.

"Well, Rolen is already so drunk off the two drinks he's had of shimmer water that he can't see straight. All your checks are with disadvantage 'til you guys get a rest in. Adrik, however, is perfectly fine." I shoot Ben a smile.

"Oh, your boy Addy is here to stay." I flex at the party. I even looked at Laura and shot her a quick wink.

"Well, I-I-I'm sma—" Rolen began, before he dropped his head on the table.

"Rolen?" I asked to the passed-out elf next to me. "Oh, come on Rolen, you can't quit on me now. We haven't even got in a fight yet!"

"Rolen, make me another constitution check." Mr. R said. Ben reached for another d20 and gave it a roll. He threw his hands up in the air.

"Natural twenty!" He shouted in excitement.

"Very nice," Mr. R said with some surprise in his face. "You hear Adrik talking to you and feel him nudging you. You're definitely drunk beyond belief, but not blackout yet."

"H-h-hey!" Rolen stammered. "Stop it you! What'sa matter with you?" he slurred out.

"Rolen," I shook the him. "It's me, Addy, your good drinkin' buddy Addy!" I shook him a little more.

"I-I-I knows who you is," Rolen slurred, trying to keep his eyes open. "Whys you have t-to shake me like this?"

"Just making sure you're still aroun'. Can't cop out on me jus' yet." I laughed.

"'Ey Bart!" Mr. R called. "Gimme another roun' for me an' me frien's 'ere, eh?" he slurred. Mr. R shifted in his chair looking to the right. "You sure about that, Benj? The elf there looks a bit finished already," he asked himself. He shifted himself again looking to his left. "Ahh keep 'im on somethin' easy eh? Mead, like me an' me brother 'ere," he slurred. "Benji reaches into his pocket and pulls out a small vial with a glimmering red liquid in it. Aye, elf boy. Down this would ya? And he hands it to Rolen."

"O-okay sure," Rolen said. He pops the top off the vial and downs the whole thing in one gulp.

"Now, how ya feelin'?" I asked.

"I don't know. How am I feeling?" Ben looked at Mr. R.

"Welp, you know what you gotta do," Mr. R responded. Ben grabbed his d20, gave it a shake in his fist, and let it loose on the table.

"Seventeen. What do I add to this?" Ben questioned.

"It was a constitution check but since it was high enough anyways, you are overcome with a warm feeling following the liquid down your throat and into your stomach. A sobering sensation comes over you. As if you hadn't had a drink at all." Mr. R told Ben.

"I-I feel, I feel great!" Rolen shouted. "Let the party continue!"

"Now that's more like it! Bartender, hit this fine man with another glass!" I told Mr. R.

"Here you guys go, another round." he responded as he set down a mug for each of you.

"At this point Lerissa and Torinn you have caught up with the gang. They are a bit drunk but nothing out of hand yet." Mr. R explained.

"I just take a seat next to the two idiots and start drinking one of their drinks they've already started," Laura said, as she began sipping on her root beer.

"I'll sit and have myself a nice glass of water if you don't mind," Torinn said. "I take a seat next to Lerissa."

"I'm gonna come out of the shadows and sit with them too," Liam said.

"Ront?" I asked. "W-where were you at this whole time?"

"Just keeping an eye out, my friend," Ront chuckled. "Bartender, I'll have whatever they've been drinking all night."

"Bart walks over to the keg he's been pouring out of and pours everyone another mug," Mr. R narrated. "So, what brings such a ragtag group as you guys into Faria?" he asked.

"Well," Lerissa chimed in. "We're not quite sure. We are heading to the Temple of the Raven Queen. No idea what we're going to find there, we just know it's in Allurena and in two days it will be open for outsiders," she explained. "The man that sent us on this mission told us that we will know what we are seeking when we see it. It wouldn't have been an issue, but the two drunks over there," Laura pointed a thumb at me and Ben, "Decided we had to sign a contract to ensure we get paid. So now we're stuck in what I'm assuming is a magically binding contract with a devil or something," she complained as she rolled her eyes and drank a bit more of her drink.

"Did you say the Temple in Allurena?" Mr. R asked sitting up in his chair. Laura's expression grew concerned.

"Yeah... why?" she questioned, raising her eyebrow.

"Come with me real quick," Mr. R said "He motions to the back room behind the bar."

"I get up from the bar and walk to the back with Bart." Laura directed.

"I'm gonna follow them into the back but stay hidden like usual," Liam said.

"Give me a stealth roll," his uncle responded. Liam reached into his dice bag and pulled out a black d20 with bright red numbers. He gave it a roll and the heavy metal die hit the foam on the table with a muffled thud. Liam began to laugh.

"Well... I rolled a two," Liam chuckled. "But with a plus thirteen to my stealth, it's a fifteen."

"Okay. You manage to stay hidden away in the shadows behind Lerissa and Bart as they walk down a hallway," Liam's Uncle described.

"Where are we going?" Lerissa asked.

"I'm taking you to Madame Reita," Bart said. "She is one of the oldest and wisest people in this town. She might be useful to you."

"Who is this Madame Reita?" Lerissa questioned again.

"Madame Reita is one of the leaders of Faria. She runs what we call the ladies of the night. Young women, mostly orphans and abandoned as children, who manipulate and extract information from patrons here in the pub. Usually high profile beings. Politicians, celebrities, wealthy people. With this information, Madame Reita holds this information as blackmail to have a position of power over these 'higher ups.'" He air quoted. "She has lived in many places around the world. Before she settled here in Faira decades ago, she lived in Allurena, doing what she does now, but in service to the Raven Queen."

"Oh," Lerissa muttered.

"You reach a door where Bart knocks three times pausing between each knock. The little slot in the door opens," Mr. R said, knocking on the table. "What do you seek? The eyes behind the door ask." He paused for a second. "I seek knowledge from the mother of the night," he responded to himself. "Bart reaches into his pocket and pulls out a coin. He takes the coin and places it into a slot in the center of the door. The coin slides into the slot perfectly. He turns the coin, and the door begins to glow with green veins of arcane light that spread from the coin slot. The door clicks and creaks open. A woman stands behind the door to greet you. She turns and leads you into the chamber."

"There in the back end of the chamber is a beautiful tiefling woman laying on a pile of pillows," Mr. R began describing to us. "Her purple skin and long tail-like horns stretch from her forehead, through her hair, and down the back of her neck to her shoulders. She has a welcoming appearance that also strikes fear into you." Mr. R ran his hands over his head to show the horns and how they reach over her head. "Her tail is folded over her leg and keeps her skirt up a bit, exposing her legs. When you all walk into the light of the room, she looks at you, and motions you closer."

"What have you brought to me, Bartholomew?" Mr. R said, his voice changing to that of an older woman; very firm but soft to the ear, welcoming and bone chilling at the same time. "I have a group of adventurers here who are on their way to your former home in Allurena," he spoke up. "And you know exactly what time of year it is, don't you Reita?" Bart questioned the lady, his voice peaking with a bit of concern.

"She steps down from her throne of pillows, her feet touching the ground so softly that is almost seems that she is floating," Mr. R describes. "She begins approaching you, Lerissa. Her menacing red eyes peering into your soul. She walks up to you and begins to study you, looking you up and down. Running a finger across your back gently, she rolls bits of your hair in between her fingers. She steps over your tail, but you feel her tail drag over yours and partially intertwine with it. She comes back in front of you and traces her sharp finger up your neck until she reaches the tip of your chin." Mr. R paused. "She leans in. Your noses almost touching. You can see every crease and wrinkle on her face. And for being a tiefling there aren't many for the age you presume her to be."

"Why does your friend skulk in the shadows behind you?" Reita asked softly. "Does he not trust me?"

"As she says that, Liam, you suddenly feel something grab you and drag you out of the shadows," Mr. R said as he made a fist and grasped at the air in front of him. "You try to fight it, but the arcane power is too much for you. It drags you along the floor and forces you to your knees in front of Madame Reita," he narrated. "Do you know what I do to people who intrude on my private meetings, young orc?" Reita asked Ront. "She reaches down and squeezes your cheeks between her thumb and middle finger, forcing you to look up at her,"

"Let me guess," Ront spoke up. "You're going to intimidate me with a threat to my life? Is that it? Well I've got some bad news for you sweetheart, I'm not shaken that easily."

"I need you to roll me an intimidation check, Liam," Mr. R instructed. Liam sat and locked scowling eyes with his uncle as he reached out to grab his metal die again.

"Eleven," Liam announced. He never broke eye contact with his uncle. It gave me chills.

"I admire your charisma, young rogue. But no, why would I kill you? You would be much more useful to me alive, wouldn't you?" Reita smiled. "But before that, what is this I hear about you going to my former home... Allurena?"

Lerissa rolled her eyes at this question. "We took a contract," she sighed. "Thanks to our barbarian and druid friends who are drinking themselves to death out there at the bar. We met a man in Tal'ireald who promised riches beyond belief. Tweedledee and Tweedledum in the next room wanted to ensure that we got the reward. So the man that they met pulled out a contract and the two idiots signed it without consulting us. So now we're bound to finishing this contract or god knows what will become of us." She shook her head. "And the temple, I'm guessing you already know, opens—"

"At the crack of dawn on the first morning of midsummer, I know all of that," Reita recited, Mr. R circling his hand in the air. "But what did this being want from the temple?"

"He never said," Lerissa said. Her face grew red with embarrassment and she bit her lip. "He told us that once we are in, we will know what we were seeking."

"Why do you care so much?" Ront asked. "What does it matter to you? It's not like you're the guardian of the temple anymore."

"Liam!" Laura yelled. I jumped almost falling out of my chair being brought back into reality. "How did you know that about her?"

"I did a one on one with Uncle Matt a few weeks ago before we left for the movies." Liam grinned. "I went and did some research on our destination. I still don't know what, or even who we are going to find inside. But I know that Reita here," Liam said as he pointed his thumb at his uncle. "She is the former guardian of the temple, before she was replaced by whoever the current guardian is." We all sat there in shock looking at Liam.

"Were you planning on sharing any of this with us?" I scolded. "Maybe before we end up getting murdered by some random woman in the back of a pub?"

"I was waiting for when we reached the black sand beaches where the temple resides," Liam said shaking his head. "I wasn't expecting us to end up here."

"So, what else do you know about the temple?" Laura asked sternly.

"Uh-uh-uh," Mr. R interjected, shaking his finger. "That's something Lerissa would have to ask Ront."

"Ugh. Okay, okay," Laura said shaking her head.

Mr. R turned his gaze back at Liam. Both of their faces went back into game mode. You could see them both building back into their characters.

"What does the former guardian care about our mission to the temple?" Ront restated in his half-orc voice.

"What you have been sent after may not be what you are expecting," Reita began to tell the two. "Deep in the temple lie many things. Items from all walks of life. Some are just artifacts." He paused. "But some of these items could release such darkness and evil upon the world! What lies buried deep inside that tomb could bring about another age of darkness to us all."

"She then turns away towards the pillow throne," Mr. R narrated. "She digs her arm deep under a layer of pillows and pulls out a glass orb." Mr. R raised his hand as if to hold up the orb himself. "She begins to tell you, back in the time before the ancients crossed from the planar gate into the world we live in today. Before man spread across the world like a disease, there were giants. The orb in her hand begins to swirl with a gray smoke inside it," Mr. R said as he began swirling his hands chasing each other around the imaginary orb. "The light gray smoke begins to darken until it's pitch black. And then out of the darkness of the orb, six images appear, each image coming into focus. You both recognize these faces from books and stories you read as children. These faces are of the six giant leaders that lived on the earth before man did. Each faction is represented in the images. The hill giants and the frost giants. Fire giants and cloud giants. Stone giants and the mighty storm giants.

These creatures lived like gods in the world," Reita continued from Mr. R's mouth. "They lived in peace for many millennia, until the fire giant leader Oculous wanted more power. He knew the uprising of man was coming and he was not going to go down without a fight. From his mountains in the south, he bred war. Plumes of smoke erupted from the insides of the mountains, blacking out the sun for most of the southern hemisphere." He began swirling his hands faster and faster.

"You watch as Reita's eyes begin to gloss over from their bright blood red, into black like the smoke from the orb. As she narrates the tale, you see the images move and show the past as if you were there witnessing it," Mr. R explained. I began to lean in so far over the table, I could feel my chair tipping forward. This was getting too good.

"Oculous began attacking the other tribes... Reita's voice begins to gain another voice behind it as she speaks. Her fingertips begin to glow red and her hair slowly begins to blow around behind her." Mr. R mimicked the hair with his hands. "He started with the hill giants of the east and the frost giants of the north. His numbers quickly grew as he gained allies in these two tribes. The stone giants told Oculous that they would not attack their own kind, but when the time came, they would aid in the fight against man...

Suddenly, Reita's eyes blast into a white light and she gains another, deeper voice, behind her other two. The room begins to swirl, and the arcane winds begin to pick up as Reita lifts off the ground." Mr. R looked up to the ceiling arms stretched out over the armrests on his wheelchair.

"In his greed, Oculous moved to the west. His armies marching in full force. But his armies were no match for the combined force of the cloud and storm giants. Swiftly, Oculous' army fell, leaving him as the last survivor. Utreil the storm giant and Timour the cloud giant, dragged Oculous beneath the sea into the tomb they created for him. They called to the Raven Queen to take Oculous' soul so they could destroy the body so that he would have no chance to return to the world. She complied with the giants, but she did not have the power to destroy the soul.

The glow in Reita's fingers begins to spread into her hands and up her arms," Mr. R said as he mimicked the actions in his chair. "You can tell that she is not alone in her mind. She stored his soul in his hammer along with the souls of his armies. The giants left and closed the temple and flooded it over with the Alluren sea. The Raven Queen knows of the power of this hammer. That is why she summons powerful beings to guard her temple in the sea, locking them inside with only one goal in mind." Mr. R paused.

"Reita then begins to float down to the ground again. The arcane winds die down and her eyes return to their original blood red," Mr. R said as he returned to his relaxed sitting pose. "Kill all those who seek the evil inside," she whispered to the room.

"And I'm going to pause you two in time for a sec," Mr. R said as he pointed at Liam and Laura. "And I'm going to check in on you guys and see what you've been up to during this whole event in the back." He looked down behind his screen. It looks like he's writing. He pulls whatever he wrote out of the binder and folds it up. He slides the paper over to Jacob. "So, Adrik, Torinn, and Rolen. You guys were last seen drinking at the bar, so give me a constitution check the two of you," he said pointing at me and Ben. It took me a second to get into the mindset of what was going on. I grabbed my die and tossed it onto the table.

"H-hey!" I cheered. "That's a nat twenty!"

"Man, I need new dice or something," Ben complained as he scanned his character sheet. "I rolled a three which comes out to a five total." Man, poor Ben. The dude hasn't rolled anything good tonight at all. And it almost killed him earlier.

"Hey, Rolen, you ol'right there?" I said in Adrik's scratchy voice.

"I-I-I," Ben stuttered. "And then Rolen just passes out onto the bar again," he narrated as he smacked his head on the table again.

"Poor boy, can't—" Benji said, followed with a hiccup. "Hol' his mead either huh? But that's elves for ya."

"Aye, every tavern we go to, Benji, every single one,' I said as I motioned at Ben who was still pretending to be passed out.

"Just then Adrik and Torinn, you notice the music that's been playing in the background since you walked into the pub," Mr. R told us. Suddenly we heard the game room fill with the sounds of tavern music. A fiddle playing a jig with a flute of some sorts. Even the chatter and murmur of patrons in a bar were in the speakers set up around the room.

"Can I roll to see if I recognize the tune?" Daryl asked as he nabbed a sparkly pink d20 out of his dice case.

"Go for it," Mr. R smiled. Daryl gave his die a toss.

"Crap!" He shouted. "Eight, nine, ten... eleven!" Daryl calculated in his head. "It's an eleven!"

"Yeah you know exactly what the tune is. And you know who is playing it," Mr. R smiled again at Daryl.

"I'm just going to get up from these two drunks and go over there to see," Torinn announced to us.

"You follow the music towards the fireplace adjacent to the entrance to the pub. There's a pretty large crowd surrounding the stage-like area in the pub. And up on stage you see your old friend Gimble playing away and dancing without a care in the world. With him on stage is a tall half-elven woman who is playing a flute or fife thing. And she's hopping around, dancing and playing with Gimble," Mr. R said. His smile was getting much larger. Pure joy shone from his face as he laid out the scene for Daryl.

"I'm going to make my way to the front and place a gold piece in the violin case that I know is set up on the front of the stage," Torinn said, with a grin.

"I'm gonna cast the spell message on the elderly dragonborn when I see him," Jacob said, winking to his brother. "Torinn! Is that you? How did you find this place?"

"One and the same, my old friend," Daryl responded in his

elderly wizard voice. "We stumbled upon this town on our way
to the black sand beaches to the west. Why are you here?"

"What kind of question is that my friend?" Gimble chuckled. "I'm a bard! I travel around the world and end up places
with no reason other than money and partners." He threw up
his hands and shrugged his shoulders. "I have so many stories
to tell you, my old friend." As he continued dancing around and
playing."

"I'm going back to Adrik and Rolen," Torinn announced.
"Addy! Have you seen who is playing tonight? Did you catch
the bard?"

"No. Why, do I know him?" I asked.

"You sure as hell should. It's Gimble!" Daryl almost couldn't
contain his excitement almost falling out of his chair.

"You're kidding?" I said trying to sound as surprised as I
could. "Where is he?"

"Up on stage," Torinn pointed. "He is playing with an elven
woman."

"Well then let's go have a watch!" I said, hoisting my root
beer in the air. "I follow Tor to the stage. I'm also gonna toss a
couple gold into the case, that I'm well aware of."

"Awesome," Mr. R said giving two thumbs up and tapping his
fists against the edge of the table. "You both pull up a couple
stools at the edge of the stage and watch Gimble finish his tune
with the other bard. The whole pub is merry and singing with
the tune. Some are even plopping small sacks of coin into the
case." He began dimming the music. "The set ends, and your
friend Gimble comes down off the stage towards you both." Mr.
R motioned a hand at Jacob.

"Tor! Addy!" Gimble called out. His accent was more Irish
and bouncy; very happy and bright as gnomes should be. It's
been quite a while since we ran into Gimble in our campaign.
Last time we had him with us we almost got murdered by an

ancient tarrasque monster, in a town named Tarrasque. But I swear I had nothing to do with waking it!

"What brings you two all the way out here in the middle of nowhere?" Gimble asked us.

"Ah, you see, my old friend," Torinn began. "We are on a mission. We are headed to the black sand beaches of Allurena to seek out the hidden temple of the Raven Queen."

"What do you mean?" Gimble questioned. His look began to grow very disconcerting. "Torinn... what do you mean you seek the hidden temple?"

"Well it's quite simple you see—" Torinn stopped.

"Hey Daryl, will you give me a perception check really quick?" Mr. R interrupted

"Oh man..." Daryl skimmed his hand around for a bit deciding which die would be the best to roll. He grabbed an orange one and a copper one. There were blues and golds. And as if god himself came down from the heavens and guided his hand, Daryl grabbed out of the center of his box and pulled out a sparkly white d20 with gold numbering. "Don't screw me now, J," Daryl said holding the die towards his brother. He took a deep breath and rolled. "Eighteen... so, twenty-one total!'

"Alright, mid-sentence explaining your predicament to Gimble, you catch a glimpse of the front entrance to the pub," Mr. R narrated. "You see a nasty-looking group of beings walk in. You hear snarling and growling. First a couple kobolds make their way into the pub. The little dragon-like creatures sniffing around and hopping up on tables. They seem to be searching for something. But following behind them is a large humanoid creature with what looks like a hellhound on a leash. As the being comes into the light of the pub, you see that the being is an orc." Mr. R began molding his face into his creature, jutting out his lower jaw and lowering his eyebrows.

"Where is the tiefling!" Mr. R growled out. "Where are they?"

Mr. R motioned as to look like he was pushing his way through crowds. "You all watch as an orc shoves his way through the small crowds inside the pub, picking up a couple halflings here and there and dropping them, or even throwing them across the room."

"Well, my friend," Torinn said as he threw up his finger. "That is a story for another time. Will you be joining us in leaving in a haste?"

"I guess I have no choice?" Gimble shrugged. "But I have to get my violin. And I begin running to the stage to grab my instrument," Jake said.

"Shall we then, Addy?" Daryl turned to me and asked. "And then I cast sacred flame on the orc." Torinn announced to the party.

"He fails," Mr. R laughed while he shook his head. "Roll your damage." Daryl reached into the compartment of shiny white die and pulled out an eight-sided die. He rolled it once, picked it back up again and rolled one more time.

"Couldn't have been any better." Daryl smiled. "Seven plus six plus seven making it a twenty total!"

"Okay. You watch as the orc suddenly bursts into flames. He's able to snuff it out, but he definitely took a bit of damage." Mr. R began to pant heavily. "Who... Who did this to Throkk?" He growled out. "Throkk begins overturning tables and throwing chairs." Mr. R threw his arms around as if he was the one throwing the furniture. "I will skin him alive!" Mr. R shouted.

4

THROUGH THE TABLE AND UNDER
THE BAR

"That would be our cue, Addy!" Torinn announced.

"But what about lightweight over here?" I asked as I pointed my thumb at Ben. "We can't leave him here passed out. He can't even walk."

"Oh alright, alright," Torinn mumbled. "I walk over to Rolen and place my hand on his back, and I cast lesser restoration."

"Rolen, you feel another bit of warmth come over you, and you begin to sober up. You also can regain half of what you lost in hit-points earlier." Mr. R said, his hands fanning himself slightly.

"W-w-what?" Rolen sputtered picking his head up off the table. "I-I'm awake! What did I miss?"

"Well, Mr. Can't-hold-his-alcohol," I began with my fists on my hips. "Somebody is here looking for our dearest frien' Lerissa, and we now need to fin' her and get out of here before we are tortured or killed! And where the hell is Gimble?"

"T-that's just g-great?" Ben said, a groggy look of confusion still on his face. His work in the theatre program at school seems to be paying off. The dude has some great acting.

"Oh, Addy, are you ready yet?" Torinn called out to us

"Coming!" I shouted across the table. "Where's Gimble?"

"Jake, I need a dex check," Mr. R requested.

"Eighteen?" Jacob looked up at Mr. R.

"Okay, you manage to make your way up to the stage and retrieve your case before barreling back through the chaotic crowd."

"Okay guys," Gimble panted. "Let's get out of here!"

"You!" Mr. R shouted as he pointed at me. "Hox! Arix! Eks! Get the dwarf and his friends!" He growled. "You guys watch as three kobolds begin moving toward you."

"Bring it! I brace for combat!" I announced. I smiled and scooped up my d20. It's time to smish a bish as I like to say.

"I guess you guys need to roll some initiative," Mr. R shrugged. Ben, Jacob, Daryl, and I grabbed our die. We all rolled our dice.

"Okay, twenty or higher?" Nobody responded. "Fifteen to twenty?" I raised my hand up. "Ten to fourteen?" Jacob and Daryl raised their hands.

"Eleven," Daryl said.

"Fourteen," Jacob followed.

"Okay," Mr. R replied as he began writing things down behind the screen. "Ben?"

"Five." He sighed. "I'm gonna die tonight aren't I?"

"Not if I have anything to say about it," I told him. I won't let him die to a measly kobold. The little runts won't get a good hit on any of us.

"Alright, Adrik, you're first." Mr. R pointed his pencil at me. He clicked a button on his laptop, and the screen in the table changed scenes. There was a battle map setup. Mr. R pulled out a handful of miniature statues from the shelf behind him. A dwarf, a half-elf, a dragonborn, a gnome, and three kobolds. He placed the four of our characters huddled together at the back of the pub and put the three kobolds in a semi-circle moving towards us. Our only escape is the hallway behind us, that Lerissa and the bartender went down.

"I'm going to move to the middle kobold," I told Mr. R. I leaned over the table and moved the Adrik mini in front of the middle of the three kobolds. Counting my spaces. Five feet, ten feet, and I stop. "And then I'm going to dual-hand my axe." I pull my hands next to my head like I'm winding up a real axe. "And I'm gonna try to split him in two down the middle!"

"Roll to hit," Mr. R nodded. I gave my d20 a nice toss onto the rubber mat of the table.

"Nineteen," I looked up at Mr. R.

"Hits." He nodded again. I picked up my twelve-sided die out of my dice line-up and rolled it.

"Eight slashing damage," I looked back at Mr. R. His eyes grew real big for second before returning to normal size. He chuckled a little and smiled.

"You take your axe up over your head." He mimed holding the axe above his own head before moving downward towards the table. "And with no resistance, you slice straight through to the floor. The kobold stands there silent and still for a moment. And then like in a cartoon, the two halves separate and fall to the ground." He put his hands together and then split them like the kobold. He then pulled himself up and reached out and set the middle kobold piece on its side. "You killed the first kobold."

"I turn to the guys covered in blood, and I say... Aye boys, they're ripe for the killin'!" I throw my arms out like Russell Crowe in *Gladiator*. "Are you not entertained?" I asked Mr. R. He smiled back at me.

"Does that end your turn?" He asked me.

"Oh no," I smiled. "I've got my second attack and some movement left. I'm gonna move to the next one. Let go with the left one. And I do the same thing." I leaned over again and moved my mini to the next kobold. Then I grabbed my d20 and rolled it. "Ouch, not as good. Thirteen?" I looked at Mr. R. He nodded at me. I grabbed the d12 and rolled it. "Nine?"

"You split another kobold in half. Not as clean as the other but you manage to slice through one shoulder and out the hip. And the kobold lets out a little 'Ack' as it's robbed of life."

"Perfect, I'll end my turn there then," I said satisfied with my two kills.

"Alright, Gimble you're up." Mr. R turned and looked at Jacob after placing another kobold on its side.

"Oh, man, let's see," Jacob said as he scratched his chin. "They seem pretty easy to kill. I guess... I'm gonna move to the last remaining kobold and stab him with my dagger."

"Roll to hit," Mr. R said to Jacob. And like me, he picked up his d20 and gave it a roll.

"Fifteen," he said looking at Mr. R.

"Hits, go ahead with damage." He nodded again. Jacob reached into his dice bag and pulled out the pyramid shaped die. A d4. He rolled the small die and watched it fly across the table.

"Whoops," he exclaimed. "That was a little harder than I meant to roll it. What did it land on, Liam?"

"Three," Liam said as he picked up the die and tossed it back at Jacob.

"So, five total," Jacob told Mr. R.

"Okay. You run at the kobold." He reached up and moved the gnome mini right to the last kobold. "You pull your dagger and plunge it into the kobold's stomach. You watch his eyes widen as you stab him. He squeals a little bit and then falls limp on your shoulder."

"Boom, that's what's up!" Jacob shouted. Throwing his hands in the air.

"You two stand over the slain kobolds." Mr. R pointed at Jacob and me. "A bit of blood on both of you. And then you hear growls and snarls around the room. The other kobolds are not happy with their brothers being slain."

"What're you gonna do about it, ya useless dragons?" I shouted at the table. I looked over at Mr. R and watched his jaw shift back into its orc form.

"Never send a worthless being to get things done," Mr. R growled. "My turn." Mr. R rolled his shoulders and sat up in his chair. "You guys watch as the orc reaches over his shoulder and pulls out a large greataxe. Much larger than Adrik's. He takes the axe and drops it through a table," he explained.

"Now, that's more like it!" I cheered. I slammed my chest and threw my arms up.

"Awesome, reroll initiative," Mr. R asked. Again, we picked up our d20's and rolled them.

"Ten," I called out.

"Eight," Jacob replied.

"Seventeen," Daryl announced.

"Sixteen," Ben said.

"Alright," Mr. R clapped his hands together and rubbed them against each other. "You guys watch as the orc begins moving in on you all, dragging his axe across the ground. But before he attacks you—" He turned and pointed at Liam and Laura. "Reita just sat down and told you about the guardian's mission. Right as she sits down on the throne of pillows, you all hear a huge crash in the bar."

"I get up and head to the door," Lerissa jumped.

"Me too!" Ront followed.

"Okay, you both jump in the air and head down the hall," Mr. R started. "But Liam, before you get through the door you feel two beings stop you. There's no one touching you, but you feel something grab you, lift you off your feet, and turn you back to Madame Reita."

"Oh great, now what?" Ront rolled his eyes.

"You snuck into my domain out of lack of trust in your friend," Mr. R said in Reita's voice. "You disrespected me and your friend there. I am giving you mercy not killing you here on my floor. But for my kindness and forgiveness, I leave you with this." He paused. "Then Reita reaches out for your arm. Unwillingly, your arm is handed to her. She turns your palm face up and places one hand over your forearm." He mimed to Liam. "You now are in my servitude. One day I shall call upon you. For what, you may never know. But you will know when I call." He clicked his laptop keyboard. "And you begin to feel a burning and a stinging sensation in the spot her hand is covering. And when she moves her hand you see a symbol burned and inked into your arm." And he gestured to the image on the table screen. The image was of a raven's head. The symbol of the Raven Queen. But the raven had horns. It must be a custom symbol of Reita or something. "You will know when the time has come. Now go, rescue your friends."

"You're insane, lady," Ront said, rubbing his arm.

"Oh, and Ront," Mr. R said in his Reita voice. "Just so you know, if I call and you don't show, you'd best hope your friends aren't around to see the gruesome end that curse will bring." He smiled as he waved off Liam.

"I head back down the hallway, pulling my hood up on my cloak of invisibility and pull out my daggers," Liam said.

"Okay, as you both head into the main bar, you see a large orc dragging his axe towards your friends who are standing in the bloody pools that were once three kobolds."

"Do I get an attack of opportunity since I'm sneak attacking the orc from outside his combat?" Lerissa asked.

"Sure. What do you want to do?" Mr. R nodded.

"I'm going to fireball with the orc as the center of the ball," Laura explained.

"Okay. I need a dex saving throw from Adrik and Gimble." Mr. R asked.

"What? Why?" I questioned.

"Fireball has a twenty-foot radius, and you two are in a twenty-foot radius from the orc," Mr. R explained while rolling a couple of dice behind his screen.

"Ugh," I groaned throwing my head back as I picked up my d20. I rolled my head to my shoulder and looked at Laura. "Why do you hate me?" She looked back, smiled, and gave me another wink. I'm not crazy, that's like the millionth and one wink she's given me tonight. Is she trying to tell me something? Gross! No! That's Ben's sister you idiot! That'd be like kissing Ben or something. N-not that I want to kiss Laura. But I mean I guess I wouldn't not kiss her if she asked... No! No! No, no, no! That's a bad thought. She's your friend's older sister. That's gotta be illegal or something. Against some form of bro code or something.

"Would you just roll already so I can kill you all faster?" Laura asked as she laughed, and winked. Again!

"Oh, r-right!" I rolled my die.

"Ten," Jacob said.

"Nineteen," I followed. Mr. R looked over at Laura.

"My spell DC is sixteen." She winced looking over at Jacob. "Sorry Jake," She placed her hand on his shoulder. "But this is gonna hurt." Laura dug her hand into her chainmail dice bag and began pulling out d6's. Poor Jacob. He's so screwed! Laura scooped up all the d6's she pulled out and gave them all a roll. The cluster spread out across the table in front of her. She counted up all her dice. "Ouch, twenty-six." She turned back to Jacob.

"Oh yeah," Jacob's voice cracked. "Just almost all my health. But I-I'm fine. This is fine." He laughed.

"Well, you cast a ball of fire that erupts from the orc's location," Mr. R described. "The ball grows and expands, engulfing the kobolds, hellhound, and Gimble. Adrik hits the deck before the flames hit him. Once the flame dies out, you see an even more burnt Throkk, three crispy kobold bodies, a toasty Gimble, and an unscathed hound. Liam, you're still invisible. Do you want to do something before joining initiative rotation?" Mr. R asked.

"Yeah," Liam replied. He pushed himself up over the lip of the table and grabbed his and Laura's minis and moved them into the doorway on the map. "I want to move around behind, Throkk?" He looked at his uncle for confirmation. Mr. R nodded. "And I want to stab him in the back of the neck." He grabbed his mini and moved it behind the orc mini.

"Roll me to hit," Mr. R requested. He grabbed his die, shook it, and rolled.

"Seventeen?" He looked to his uncle.

"Hits, roll damage," Liam pulled out his tan dice bag and began searching for d6's too. He grabbed a handful of them with a d4 in the pile and gave them a roll. The dice scattered and Liam grouped them all back together. He looked up and began calculating his numbers.

"Two, fourteen, twenty, twenty-two, thirty, thirty-five total," Liam calculated.

"Okay," Mr. R sat up. "You sneak around the group and Throkk. You get up behind him and bury your dagger into the side of his neck. Blood begins to spurt out of his wound. Give me a dex save to avoid getting blood on you." Liam rolled his d20.

"Fourteen," he said.

"You avoid the blood and manage to stay hidden away," Mr. R told him. "Throkk spins around and takes a swing at the air behind him blindly. Make me another dex check, and then you and Laura make me an initiative roll."

Liam grabbed his dice and rolled, picked it back up and

rolled a second time. "Eighteen on the dex. Twelve on the initiative," Liam said. Laura rolled her die.

"Seventeen." She looked at Mr. R.

"Okay cool. You all watch as Throkk spins in anger, blindly swings at the air behind him and breaks through one of the support beams next to him." Mr. R mimicked swinging and being angry. "Agh! I will slaughter you all!" Mr. R roared. "And he's going to turn around and slam down on Adrik." Mr. R rolled a die behind the screen. "Does a twenty-two hit?"

"Oh, yeah it does," I responded laughing at the question.

"You take thirteen slashing damage," Mr. R told me.

"Is tha' all ya got?" I shouted at the orc. "My grandmother is two-hundred and seventy-five, and she does more damage than tha'!" I taunted the orc.

"After Throkk attacked you, Adrik, the hellhound makes its move on you." Mr. R stopped and rolled a die. "Eighteen hits?"

"Yeah," I sighed. Mr. R rolled another die behind the screen.

"Okay, this time you take fourteen damage as the hound leaps at you and buries its teeth into the holes in your armor. The bite both stings and burns from the bite and the fire damage from the fire inside the hound."

"Argh!" I shouted. "Bloody hell, tha's more like it!" I pounded my chest with my fist—and then rubbed the spot I hit because I hit myself too hard. Laura giggled after that. I'm definitely blushing a little. I can feel it in my cheeks.

"Alright, Torinn you're up." Mr. R announced.

"Oh, thank god," Daryl said in relief. "I'm going to walk over to Gimble, place my hands on his shoulder, and I'm going to cast cure wounds at third level." Daryl grabbed his white d8 and rolled it three times. "You regain twenty-two hit points," Daryl told his brother.

"Ah, you're such a life saver old friend!" Gimble told Torinn with a smile.

"And that's my turn," Daryl said.

"Okay, back to Lerissa," Mr. R said gesturing to Laura.

"I'm going to run at Throkk and hit him with my staff." She paused and rolled her die. "I'm guessing a ten does not hit?" She asked wincing again.

"Sadly, my dear, it does not," Mr. R replied. "Rolen, you're up."

"Oh, man, this'll be somethin'." Ben chuckled. "Let's see. I'm gonna cast thorn whip." He paused and rolled his d20. "Does a twenty hit?" he asked.

"Yeah, was that a natural twenty or non-natural?" Mr. R questioned.

"Non-natural," Ben replied. He picked up his d6 and gave it three rolls. "Twenty on damage as well," Ben smirked.

"You all watch as a whip covered in thorns spawns from Rolen's wrist, kind of like Spiderman. The whip wraps itself around Throkk's chest and drags him to the floor and over to Rolen. He looks up at you from the floor and says 'You will regret killing me! Death's Hand will find you! They will kill you before you reach the temple of our Queen of Death.' and he spits at you." Mr. R paused. "And then he slowly fades before finally choking on the blood in his mouth that trickled down his cheek onto the floor."

"Great, now we have something called Death's Hand after us?" Ben asked the group.

"Ront, you're up," Mr. R pointed at Liam.

"Wait, isn't it over—" He stopped himself mid-sentence. "Oh, right the hellhound. Um," he hummed in thought for a second. "I'm gonna take my dagger and throw it at the hound's face. Aiming for his eye." Liam rolled. "Twenty-two has to hit?" he asked.

"It hits," Mr. R said. Liam grabbed his d4 and began shaking it around in his hand.

"Since I'm still invisible do I get a sneak attack?" Liam asked.

"Yeah, since he can't see you, I'll say you get a sneak." Mr. R shrugged. Liam grabbed his pile of d6's from the last attack and rolled them in his hands. He let them loose in front of him. "Thirty-six piercing damage."

"You all watch as a dagger comes from out of nowhere, next to the smashed support beam, and flies across the room. It impales itself deep inside the hound's eye, blinding him in one eye," Mr. R said pointing at his eye.

"And then I want to move across the room and get on the bar," Liam directed.

"Okay, Adrik. Your turn." Mr. R pointed at me.

"I'm gonna kill the little bugger that bit me!" I exclaimed. "I'm gonna bury my axe in his head." I rolled. "Twenty-seven hits," I say as I begin rolling my damage. "Twelve slashing damage."

"Like the game at the carnival, you drag your axe above your head and drop it on the hound's head. Splitting open the head and splattering blood all over," Mr. R described. "You guys stand in the middle of this destroyed pub, that you now realize is empty. You're standing in a pool of blood with destroyed corpses lying around. What do you guys want to do from here?"

5

ANSWERS IN THE LIGHT

"What else?" I asked. "I'm looting the bodies."

"Who all is looting, then?" Mr. R asked. Everyone raised their hands. "Okay, give me investigation checks." We all rolled our dice.

"Six," I said.

"Natural one," Jacob sighed.

"Sixteen," Liam smiled.

"Fifteen," Daryl said.

"Eighteen." Ben shot a smile at Liam.

"Ten," Laura rolled her eyes.

"Alright," Mr. R said. "Ront, Torinn, Rolen, and Lerissa, you each find about twenty gold each. There's also a couple of weapons laying around. A couple of short swords, some daggers, and the great axe. But Rolen," Mr. R pointed at Ben. At the same time, he slid his other hand over to me and handed me a folded piece of paper. "You find a journal inside Throkk's bag. It's a leather-bound book with a strap around it to keep it closed." Mr. R pulled out the exact book he described to us and handed it to Ben. He took the book and began undoing the strap wound around the book.

"There's an inscription on it," Ben said as he ran his hand over the cover. "But I don't know what this says. Do I know this language?" he asked Mr. R.

"Well, what languages do you know?" Mr. R replied.

"Umm..." Ben hummed as he started looking through the other papers in his binder. "Ah here!" He slammed his finger on the page. "Common, Elvish, Druidic, Undercommon, Sylvan, and Draconic."

"Well, it's in Underdark," Mr. R said. "The cover reads '*Death's Hand*' on it. Under that, it says 'Throkk the Bloody',"

"I'm gonna read it," Ben told us as he opened the book in his hands.

"When you open it to the first page you read 'Orders' at the top. The next bit reads '*Throkk. You are to seek out the tiefling named Lerissa, and her party. You are to kill them all except her. She is to be brought alive to me. If she is not, you will join her party in death. You must get her before she reaches the temple in Allurena. Signed Barakas*'," Mr. R read out.

"Umm," Ben mumbled. "Lerissa, you might want to have a look at this. And I hand the book to her." He handed the book over to Laura to read. Her expression exploded in shock.

"Tell me I'm not reading this extra bit you missed?" She asked.

"What do you mean?" Ben asked confused. "I read everything in the book."

"But what's all this under it?" She shouted as she turned the book around. It looked pretty simple. There wasn't anything more than a small paragraph with a title over it that I'm assuming is the '*Orders*' written up top. "Right here!" She pointed at the bottom of the page. But it was blank.

"Are you okay Laura?" I asked. Maybe she was going crazy. I mean it would make sense after all the winking and stuff. But I'm guessing by her reaction that she didn't like that question.

"I'm perfectly fine," she argued. "Come here and look at the book!" I stood up and went to stand behind her to look at what she was seeing. "Wait!" She shouted at the book. "Where'd it all go?" I picked up her root beer and gave it a sniff.

"Is there something in here?" I asked.

"No, you idiot!" She yelled at me. "I swear there was way more in here a second ago. Paragraphs and paragraphs. And there were runes everywhere too! I swear I'm not losing it!" She sat and examined the book more. Flipping pages, turning it upside down, she even tried heating the page up by breathing on it. She then picked up her own root beer and gave it a sniff. "There isn't anything in here is there, Matt?"

"I don't touch the sodas except to get them in my fridge," Mr. R laughed. "You okay though? Do you need a sec before we move on?"

"No... no, I'm fine," Laura sighed. "I could've sworn that the book had way more to it."

"Well," Mr. R shrugged. "They always say read between the lines," he smiled. Maybe she wasn't crazy. Maybe Mr. R was messing with her. Then again, I've heard rumors that some women have this mental illness called pissed at men syndrome. I have no idea what it is, but I'm scared she might be falling down that path. If she is sick with this disease, we might not be able to keep playing with her.

"This has your tricky hands all over it, Matt." Laura pointed at Mr. R. "I just know it!" That too might be true. He has been known to do some crazy tricks before. He once sold Adrik what he claimed was the egg of a great beast. Even gave me a real egg that was gold and covered in gems. When I carried it for months, I finally asked him when it will hatch. One of his non-playable characters (or NPC) took the egg and cracked it into a hot pan. It was a chicken egg painted gold. I spent over a thousand gold on that egg!

"You may never know," Mr. R smiled as he rolled his dice behind the screen. "So, you guys loot the bodies and find some items."

"I'm taking all the weapons and putting them in the bag of holding," Liam interrupted.

"Okay. After you guys take what you found, you hear someone speak up from behind the bar." Mr. R ducked down a little, hiding behind the table. "A-are they gon'?" It was Benji!

"Benji?" I asked. "Benji, w-why are you hidin' behind the bar?"

"Because." He hiccupped. "I wanted to see you lot fight, but I wanted to stay alive too!"

"But what abou' all those war stories? Like when you single-handedly fought off Torr the Defiler's army and took 'im prisoner?" I questioned.

"Oh yeah, all true!" He hiccupped again. "But wha' can I do without Eldrith?"

"Who's Eldrith?" I moved closer.

"Eldrith." Another hiccup. "Why she's my faithful 'ammer! I left 'er at home like I always do. Nobody ever come in 'ere like tha'!" Then Mr. R put his fingers in between his teeth and gave a loud high pitched whistle. He stuck his hand out in front of himself. And from behind us, and almost hitting Daryl and Ben, a toy hammer came flying into Mr. R's hand. "This, my frien's, is Eldrith!" And he planted a kiss on the head of the hammer.

Looking closer at the prop I could see that there was a piece of fishing line on the bottom of the hammer's handle. It went all the way to the ceiling. How did we not see it before?

"Okay, that's too cool!" Daryl shouted.

"Aye, she's been with me since the battle of the great gates of Loderr. Through the pits of Torog. And even to my final battle when we stormed the slave mines of Dracomear," he said hoisting the hammer high over his head.

"The slave mines?" Torinn asked. "My friend, that was well over one hundred years ago. Long before even I was around. How old did you say you were again?"

"Ah, I'm nearly two hundred and thirty years old at this point. You begin to lose count after the first hundred." He laughed. "I was one of the front men, riding my war pig into battle. I stormed the cave entrance, and with Eldrith by my side, I managed to free hundreds of thousands of enslaved beings."

"That is quite remarkable," Torinn said with excitement. "I've never met anyone who fought that battle. My grandfather had been in the grand army, but he had taken an arrow to the shoulder before your army got close enough."

"This is nice and all," Lerissa interrupted. "But I have a death cult thing hunting me down. So, if you two are done, I'd like to get some answers."

"W-what happened in here?" Mr. R shouted. That must be Bart.

"We were attacked while you were in the back there. An orc and a bunch of kobolds from something called Death's Hand," I explained.

"They were here looking for Lerissa!" Torinn called out.

"Do you know anything about this?" Mr. R asked over his shoulder. "This is not good, that's what I know," he responded to himself in Reita's voice.

"Well, obviously, it's not good!" Lerissa shouted at Reita. "They want me at any cost! What do they want with me?"

"My dear—" Reita started.

"Oh don't '*My dear*' me!" Lerissa interrupted. "I want answers! Why does some cult named Death's Hand want me? What could I possibly offer to them?"

"Your magic," Reita said, soothingly.

"What about it?" Lerissa snapped back.

"We share a lot, you and I," Reita told her. Lerissa's face

began to grow more confused than angry but remained scrunched with anger. "I was fairly young when I learned the truth about who I was and could become."

"What are you talking about?" she asked again.

"You and I are powerful magic users," Reita sighed. "Powerful in necromancy. The magic of life, death, and the undying."

"So what?" Lerissa challenged. "This death cult wants me to use my magic to revive or kill someone?"

"It's more than that my dear," Reita mumbled. "They want your magic for so much more. They seek an army. Hundreds of thousands of soldiers. An army of undead beings."

"I'm nowhere near having that ability though."

"They don't care. They will force you into it. They will torture you and corrupt you until you raise a grand army."

"But why do they need an army?" I asked.

"Death's Hand is a radical religious group who worship the Raven Queen," Reita began. "They believe killing those deemed unworthy or inferior will please the Raven Queen. They believe any practice in death will please her. So, raising an army from the dead, and taking over the world, is high on their list." He put his hand up high showing the ranks of this so-called list.

I was not expecting radical cults. I thought this was a normal snatch and grab. Not a whole world domination plot. But I wanna know, why are they just now going after Lerissa? Why now?

"So, this group wants to destroy the world, and they need my magic and power to get there? What's to stop me from killing myself then?" Lerissa asked.

"They are," Reita answered. "How do you think they found you? They've been watching over you ever since you cast your first spell. They've known every step you have taken. And if you were even to try to take your own life they would stop you before you could even think it."

"So, I have a bunch of crazed stalkers... I thought I finished high school." Laura rolled her eyes. "At least this time they aren't in my window at home and are watching from afar."

"What if we did it?" Rolen questioned. "What if one of us were to kill her? Or she was killed by another being?"

"If they can stop her from harming herself," Mr. R pointed at Laura "Then they can stop you. And unlike with her, they won't be merciful to you."

"What are we supposed to do, then?" Lerissa asked.

"Continue on your journey west." Reita pointed. "Find the sea town of Allurena. From there, seek out the great wizard Dorn the Bright. He may be able to help you beyond what I could do for you, my child. Now hurry! They will send more after you all once they learn about Throkk's death."

"But what about you guys?" Rolen asked. "They will surely come back here in their chase of us."

"Don't fret my friends," Reita said. Mr. R turned and motioned a hand behind himself. "Bart here has a special party trick up his sleeve for them." He turned back to us. "Now go! Fly, you fools!"

"I guess we head west, then?" Daryl surveyed the group.

"Let's go!" I shouted. Everyone nodded in agreement.

"Alright you all make your way to the edge of town and begin heading to the west," Mr. R recited.

"Can I look for a couple of horses on the outskirts?" Liam asked his uncle.

"Give me a perception check," Mr. R responded.

"Eighteen plus six, so twenty-four," Liam calculated.

"You see three horses tied down outside the town," Mr. R explained. "Not abandoned, mind you. Just tied down for the night."

"I want to untie them and take them for us," Liam said

"Okay," Mr. R responded clicking his tongue in thought.

"Give me a..." He trailed for a moment. "Let's make it an animal handling check."

"Seventeen," Liam looked at his uncle.

"Okay. You manage to untie the horses without spooking them and bring them to your party." Mr. R detailed.

"So, we have three horses here, and there are six of us," Ront explained to the group. "I'm gonna say we put one halfling on a horse with me and one with Rolen. Are you okay keeping an eye on Torinn?" he asked Lerissa.

"Why don't you babysit Grandpa this time?" She shot back. "You're strong enough to pick him up if he falls off. I'm going to ride with Adrik." She said. And without skipping a beat, she winked again at me. This time I didn't get all flustered and heated. My chest was beating a little faster but nothing awful. She must have desensitized me, winking at me so much. And like the stud I am, I shot her back a wink.

Now I'm blushing again. I could feel the blood rush to my cheeks and my chest beat even faster. Bad idea! Bad idea! "So, uh, Lerissa and I on a horse." My voice cracked and squeaked. "Then?" I said high pitched before coughing to clear my throat. "Me and Lerissa then?" I asked again this time dropping my voice to avoid cracking.

"Whatever." Liam rolled his eyes. Daryl and Ben also rolled their eyes at the idea too. But I could really care less. I'm on a horse with Laura. Wait, no, that's wrong! Ick! Why would I even like that idea? No, I've never had a dream about her and me on a horse before. I definitely wasn't a dwarf, and she wasn't a demon woman thingy. Never happened.

"Alright. You all mount your horses with your riding buddy and take off. Are you guys just riding straight to Allurena?" Mr. R asked. "Or would you like to stop mid-way and break for a rest?"

"If we ride there can we count it for a rest?" Ben asked.

"I'll say you could take a short rest on horseback if you ride straight through the night," Mr. R responded.

"I'm cool with going straight there," Ben said, surveying the group.

"I say we ride through," Laura said. "We still need to fulfill that contract you idiots signed. And we can get both things done while we're there."

"So straight through the night?" Mr. R polled.

"Why not?" Jacob said. "I jump on my horse and ask Rolen, 'You coming, my friend?' And I'll throw out my hand."

"I reach up to his hand and climb on the horse," Ben proclaimed.

"Okay, Grandpa," Ront turned to Torinn. "Let's get a move on!"

"Have I ever told you about the time—" Torinn started.

"Save it for the ride," Ront interrupted. "I know I'm gonna hear it again." He rolled his eyes. "Then I get Torinn up on the horse and then pull myself up, too."

"Adrik, are you coming?" Lerissa asked. She had her hand out towards me. I reached across the table and clasped my hand with hers.

"Let's ride!" I shouted. "And then Adrik hoists himself onto the horse."

"Alright, you guys are all mounted and moving. You head out west into the dark of night," Mr. R began narrating. "You all take your turns on who takes the reins of the horse so the other may rest. After many hours of travel, the six of you crest a hill as the sun breaks across the horizon behind you, and there at the shore is a town. The town of Allurena. You can see the black sands that meet the deep blue waters crashing on the shore. Bits of lighter sands intermingle with the black sands as the water retreats. In the water, you can see lots of ships and boats. Some look official, some beaten and on the verge of sinking." Mr. R clicked his laptop, and the screen changed. There on the screen was the town of Allurena. "There are buildings much taller than those you saw in Faria. Some three, four, even five levels tall. As a breeze blows at you all, there's a mix of smells. A bit of ocean spray mixed with bread baking and meats smoking. And this is where we will take a quick break."

"Oh, thank god!" Daryl blurted out as he ran out of the room.

6

BATHROOM BREAK

As Daryl ran out of the room, I stood up and stretched. Everything popped. My shoulders, knuckles, knees, back, and elbows. I sounded like a bag of pop rocks. I went to grab my plate and the empty soda can, and as I looked up... Bam! Laura was stretching. I lost all functionality. She stretched her arms up over her head, and her shirt came up a little bit. Her stomach exposed. Why did that stop me in my tracks? It's just a stomach. A flat, toned, stomach. No! Stop it! That's Ben's sister! Stop being a perv! She's way too old for me any ways. She's literally an adult.

Then she turned around so she wouldn't hit the table. She bent over and touched her toes. And that was where I think I broke. All of a sudden my legs stopped working, and I collapsed back into my chair. What the hell is wrong with me? I've never felt like this in my life. And then I was knocked out of my trance with a swift punch in my shoulder. "Ow!" I shouted as I grabbed my arm. I looked to see who it was... It was Ben.

"Dude, that's my sister!" he whispered sternly at me making sure Laura didn't hear it. "Stop staring. It's getting creepy."

I nodded in response. "Sorry."

"Come on you idiot. I need more pizza. And by the looks of that plate, you need some too." He grabbed my arm and dragged me to the kitchen. I tried to turn and catch another glimpse of Laura, but she was already gone.

"What the hell, dude!" Ben blurted. "What is with you tonight?" He asked as he pulled the pizza from the oven. "You realize she's way too old for you, right? She's nineteen. Even if she did like you, I'm pretty sure it would be illegal."

"W-what? Oh, gross man!" I scoffed. "You think—you think I like your sister?" I fake chuckled. "Real funny. That's insane."

"Calm down. I don't care that you like her. I figured eventually one of you losers would," He laughed.

"You've got the wrong idea, Ben. Laura's nice and all, but I mean come on that'd be like kissing you." I can definitely feel the blood flood my cheeks.

"So, you've thought about kissing her, huh?" He turned and shot me a smug smile.

"W-what?" I stuttered. "N-no! No!" I pointed at him.

"Dude, it's cool. Your secret's safe with me," he assured me. He put his hand on my shoulder. "We're at that age now. We like women. Or men if that's something you're into. You can tell me you like my sister. It's not like you can do anything about it anyway."

"This is really weird. I don't have a crush on Laura," I tried to lie. It can't be that obvious. Wait, what am I saying... ugh I'm so confused.

"I'll believe that when you stop going completely brain dead when she looks at you." He laughed. "You can tell me. In fact, if you admit to me you have a crush on my sister..." He leaned in. "I'll tell you who I have a crush on. Deal?" He stuck his hand out. I took his hand and shook it. I drew a deep breath.

"Okay, I admit that I have a crush on your sister," I let out. And you know what? It felt really good to say. Like taking my backpack off again. I looked at Ben... his face had a malicious smile on it. "What?" I asked. But before I could get a response he ran around me. I turned to chase him and was stopped cold in my tracks. And there in the doorway stood Laura. "Oh god. Did you..." I tried to mutter through my suddenly dry throat. My stomach just dropped to the floor. "You didn't hear any of that did you?" I pointed behind me. I think the room just got hot, because man, am I sweating.

"Hear what?" She smiled. "The part where you admitted to my brother that you have a crush on me? Or the part where he totally just baited you into this situation and leaving after he saw I heard you?" she laughed.

"B-both I guess," I stuttered. This is what nightmares are made of. I looked down real quick and assured myself I at least had my pants on.

"I kinda figured you did," she told me. My heart began to beat even faster in my chest. "You get so lost and red when I wink at you. It's cute."

"You think... I'm... cute?" I tried to manage between breaths of—oh, wait this isn't embarrassment anymore. I legitimately cannot breathe!

"Jack?" Laura asked concerned.

"In-" I gasped. "-haler!"

"Oh god! Where is it?"

"Back-" I gasped for more air. "-pack!" My lungs felt small and on fire. I bent down and set myself on the floor. I rolled onto my back and threw my hands over my head. I started to hear myself wheezing every time I took a breath. And with every wheeze, my lungs burned more and more. Laura came running back in with my inhaler. Mr. R and Jacob following behind her with worried looks. She popped off the white cap on the mouth piece and handed it to me. I quickly put it in my mouth and gave as big an inhale as I could as I pressed down the canister. My lungs began to feel as if they were opening up. I took another puff and then laid there to breathe for a second.

"Are you okay?" Mr. R asked. "Do I need to call 9-1-1?"

"I'm good," I assured him. I sat up against the cabinet and put my hands on my head. "Just need a moment to breathe."

Laura slammed into me and hugged me tightly. "You scared me there!"

"You sure you're good?" Mr. R asked again.

"Yeah, I'll be fine." I gave him a thumbs up.

"Okay. Take it easy for a sec. No hurry," he told me before he and Jacob turned and left the room.

"I guess," I said before taking in a deep breath. "You could say you... took my breath away..." I wheezed through a smile before taking my inhaler again.

"You shit!" she scolded. "You had me worried to death that I actually killed you!"

"You and me both."

"Well, I'm gonna let you recover from almost beating us to the Raven Queen." She got up to her feet. "You want me to leave you something to drink at the table when you get back?"

"Can you grab me another root beer?"

"Sure thing, kiddo." She smiled and turned away. "Oh, and Jack," she turned back and squatted next to me. "It's cool and all that you have a crush on me. But remember that I'm nineteen. So, for me, any relationship beyond friendship with you is illegal," She placed her hand on my shoulder. "But hey, when you're older—that is if you still have this silly crush on me—maybe I'll let you take me on a date or something." She leaned in and kissed me on the cheek. The freakin' cheek! That's only centimeters from my lips! She stood up and finally walked away.

I put my hand over the spot she kissed me. I began to hear myself wheeze again and quickly took a puff from my inhaler again. I just got told that one day there's a chance that I could date Laura! She's totally into me.

"Jack!" I heard the guys shout out.

"Down here!" I called.

"Dude!" Daryl slid across the floor into the cabinet next to me. "Mr. R told us you just had an asthma attack. Are you alive?" he asked as he began poking me.

"No, I'm dead. Laura used her magic and brought me back. I'm undead now." I pushed him away.

"What happened?" Liam asked. I felt like a celebrity with all these questions.

"I just kinda had an attack. I was talking to Laura, and suddenly I just couldn't breathe." I explained.

"So..." Daryl looked around at all of us. "She took your breath away?" Ben socked him right in the shoulder.

"Dude, that's my sister!" Ben scolded him. "But really though, are you okay?" Ben turned to me and asked.

"Yeah, I'm great," I responded. And behind Ben, Liam and Daryl were mimicking what I'm guessing was making out. And boy did they really not know how. They had tongues everywhere. I pretty sure Daryl even licked the inside of his nose. I nudged Ben. He turned just in time to catch them both. And gave them both a punch in the chest.

"Come on guys. Have some respect for my sister," Ben scolded again.

"Sorry." They both bowed their heads in shame.

"Besides, she could do way better than this loser," Ben said as he jumped up and ran back to the game room. I went to sit up and follow him, but Liam stopped me.

"So like—did you two—you know? Make out?" he whispered.

"What? No!" I punched him.

"Ow! Stop that. I'm gonna have a bruise," Liam said.

"Just get out of here," I said as I pushed him off me so I could get up. "I'll be in there in a sec. I need to grab more pizza."

"Alright, Casanova," Liam said, as he ran out of the kitchen. I went over to the oven and pulled out the box with my name on it. I snagged a few slices and slid them on my plate which was on the counter. I closed the box and placed it back into the oven. As I turned back to grab my pizza, I turned around into Daryl. I nearly jumped out of my pants.

"Daryl, what are you doing?" I said. He put a finger to his lips. He pointed his index fingers at each other and spun them around each other. It took me a second to realize he was telling me to use sign language. So, I signed to him, *What are you doing?*

Did you guys... He paused, waiting for an answer. *Did you two kiss?*

I looked at him with what I was hoping was enough of an annoyed face to hide my smile. *No, she's too old for me! Plus, that's like kissing Ben. That's sick!*

Oh really? Then what's this? He pointed at my cheek, right at the spot where Laura kissed me. I pulled out my phone and turned on the camera. And there it was, a very faint lipstick mark on my cheek. She freaking branded me! And they all saw it! Crap, crap, crap, crap! I ran over to the sink and turned it on. I began scrubbing my cheek.

"Oh man!" I began whining. I turned back around to Daryl and pointed at the spot. "Is it gone?"

Yes, he signed. I grabbed some napkins and dried my face off. That was a close call! I almost died once tonight from embarrassment. I don't know how many more of those chances I'll have.

"Let's go. They're probably sitting already waiting for us," I said. Daryl nodded and headed back to the game room. I grabbed my pizza and a root beer from the fridge and made my way to the room.

I went to put my soda in the cup holder, and it clinked against another can. I forgot Laura grabbed me a soda. Well, guess that means I don't have to get up and grab my next one. I sat down, placing the soda in my hand under my chair. I skimmed my character sheet. Everything seemed current. Haven't used any rages yet and I'm only down a few hit points. I think I'll manage.

I grabbed the piece of paper Mr. R had slipped to me when we searched those Death's Hand freaks. It was a small square of paper that was laminated. When I turned it over, I read the yellow strip with black letters on the top.

Berserker Axe

No freaking way! This was the loot I managed to get from that orc? I read more.

Requires attunement

You gain a +1 bonus to attack and damage rolls made with this weapon.

Curse: *When attuned you are unwilling to put the axe down and have disadvantage with any other weapon. When attacked, you make a DC 15 wisdom saving throw. On a fail, you go berserk.*

This is crazy. Kinda scary, but awesome too. I think I might get this attuned.

"Hey Jack," Ben called to me. I looked up at him. "What's that on your cheek?" he pointed at his face.

"What?" I felt my face.

"Looks like lipstick?" he mocked. I shot a glare at Daryl who was hiding his snickering face. I looked around the room and whispered at Ben.

"Shut up, penis breath!" The smile dropped from his face.

"Man, not cool using my favorite movie against me!" Ben whined. "But really, who left a kiss on your face there, Jack? Was it your mom?" he snickered.

"You wish," I retorted.

"Oh, he really does," Laura chimed in.

"Shut up, Laura. Nobody asked you," Ben scowled at his sister.

"Weren't you supposed to tell him your crush since he told you his?" Laura smiled.

"Just shut up!" Ben began to get really red.

"Come on, Ben, you both shook on it." She giggled. "Or should I tell him?"

"Just stop, Laura!" Ben shouted at her.

"Well, you need to hold up your end of the bargain here." She smiled. "I'm just being Jack's lawyer."

"I'm not gonna…" Ben started before Laura cut him off.

"He's had a crush on your mom for the longest time."

"Dude!" Ben and I both shouted.

"My mom?" I laughed.

"Well yours is Laura!" He tried in rebuttal.

"Yeah, so?" I replied. "She's only a few years older than me. My mom is like twenty-something years older than you. My crush on Laura is a little more reasonable. I mean, by all means man, like who you want. But why my mom?"

"I don't have to tell you!" Ben pouted.

"Dude, it's cool. I really don't care. I just think it's a little weird." I tried to cheer him up. But I mean, come on, that's a little strange. I mean, that's my mom!

"Can we just drop this? I'm sorry I made fun of the lipstick on your cheek. Go wash it off so we can play when those two get back here." I nodded and went back into the kitchen. I pulled out the dish sponge and loaded it with soap. I scrubbed my cheek until it was raw this time. Then I went back in and sat down. Mr. R and Jacob still weren't back yet. So, I just sat there organizing my dice. And then I felt my phone vibrate. It was my mom texting me

-WHAT HAPPENED?

-I'm fine.
-Just got a little excited.
-Nothing to worry about.

-100% you're okay?

-Yes mom, I'm fine.

-NOW YOU'RE gonna carry your inhaler?

-Yes ma'am.

-PROMISE me you'll be careful?
-I don't want any surprises!
-Like a surprise trip to the ER.

-I promise.

-GOOD,
-So how's the game going?
-Kill anything yet?

-Yeah!

-We found a town and settled in the bar.
-Laura and Liam went and learned about our mission.
-An orc and a bunch of kobolds tried to kill us.
-We slayed them out.
-Now we're learning Laura is able to raise
the dead, and people want that power for evil.

-Ooh, Scary!

-Yeah, But Adrik's not scared.
He's not smart enough to be afraid. Haha

-Don't sell him short! He's a strong warrior.
I would know, I raised him. ;)

-Haha. How's the bar going?

-Eh, kinda slow for a Friday night. But I've got a nice
gentleman here who is
chatting with me about DnD.
He used to play back when he was your age.

-That's awesome!

-Ask him what edition he played

-HE SAYS he played 1st edition.

-When they came out with AD&D?
-No way! That's awesome!

-HE TOLD me he lived in Lake Geneva, Wisconsin.

-MOM!
-Did he know Gary Gygax?

-HE SAYS YES...
　-Ran into him all the time.

-No way!

-That's amazing! Keep him happy mom!
-VIP at the bar!

-WILL DO SWEETIE!
　-I love you! Be careful please!

-Love you too mom. I will.

-THE GENTLEMEN SAYS ROLL WELL!

-I'll do my best! Have fun mom!

I PUT my phone back down. Just imagine the things that guy saw. He was living down the street and growing up in the heart of role-playing games and their creation. I could only imagine what that was like. Back when it was all pen and paper. No TV screens in tables, or surround sound speakers set up to an iPad.

The adventures he went on. He probably went through the Tomb of Horrors in its original form. I wish I could have met this guy. Just to sit and talk adventures. What his characters were like, where they went, all that jazz. Just get in the mind of a true veteran.

"Oh, you guys are ready?" Mr. R wheeled into the room. "Sorry for making you guys wait. Jake and I were catching up." He moved himself into his spot at the table. "Everyone good?" he asked the group. He focused on me when he asked. I nodded. "Everyone got enough pizza?" Again, he focused on me. I nodded again.

"Because we got a rest, can we regain some hit points?" Ben asked.

"Please!" Jacob pleaded.

"Yeah, use your hit dice," Mr. R said. "Refresh and reset things."

I rolled one of my hit die to regain health. And it helped me regain the ten hit points I was missing.

"Now then," Mr. R clapped his hands together. "Shall we continue?"

7

ALLURENA

"You all crest the hill and see the sights of Allurena. You can see the black sand beaches on the other side of town. The scent of bread baking, and meat smoking wafts in the breeze," Mr. R described, fanning the air and smelling it. "The growing sunlight is creeping over the town and reflecting off the sea."

"Shall we make our way into the town?" Lerissa asked. "And without an answer, I steer the horse forwards to the town," Laura narrated.

"Well, that answers where I'm going then," I joked.

"We're following suit," Ront announced.

"Tally-ho!" Torinn said, in his old man voice.

"Well, Gimble?" Ben asked Jacob.

"What are you waiting for?" Gimble demanded. "And I slap the horse's ass!" Jacob laughed.

"Alright. You all head off towards the town," Mr. R said. "The four of you are trotting along the road when suddenly Gimble and Rolen blow past you in a full gallop. Ben, will you make me a strength check."

"Oh God..." Ben looked up before burying his face in his

arms. He grabbed the die and turned it towards us to show a one. "That's a natural one."

"Oh man," Mr. R sighed out. He began rolling some dice behind his screen and was writing things down, erasing them and rewriting. "Okay, as Gimble slaps the horse, you go to hold on tight, and slip; your foot caught in the harnessing of the horse. Getting dragged by the horse at full gallop you take—" he paused to scan his notes. "Thirty piercing damage, by the time the horse finally stops in the town," Mr. R said, trying to hide his guilty smile.

"Oh, you have to be kidding me!" Ben threw his hands in the air. "I'm supposed to be the nature guy who is loved by all creatures. I'm the druid, dang it!"

"When you guys reach the town, you notice that the whole town is up and about. Hustle and bustle. People are running and shouting. Carriages are racing through the streets to make their deliveries." Mr. R clicked his keyboard again, and the screen in the table shifted to a picture of a busy sea town. He gave the keyboard another click, and the speakers around the room began to play the sounds of chatter and carriages. This was pretty impressive sound work, even for Mr. R standards.

"We need to find Dorn," Laura said scanning her notes.

"And how exactly do you plan on doing that?" Liam asked.

"Let's start with this," Jacob suggested. "I'm gonna walk up to the first person I see."

"Alright," Mr. R responded. "What do you say?"

"Excuse me," Jake called putting his hand up in the air. "Excuse me, can you help us?"

"What?" Mr. R snapped. His face distorted. One eye was opened wide, and the other squinted. His jaw was pushed out and to the left a bit. He looked quite crazy.

"I'm looking for someone who lives here in this town. I was

hoping you could point me in the right direction,' Gimble explained.

"Oh sure, sure," Mr. R smiled. "But it'll cost ya." He rubbed his fingers and his thumb together,

"Oh, umm." Gimble rubbed the back of his head. "Hey, Lerissa, can I borrow some money?"

"What? No!" she shouted. "I'm not getting swindled by this lunatic!"

"Don't you want to find what's-his-name?" I asked.

"Look around," Lerissa responded. "There's a ton of people in this town walking about. We can find someone who isn't scum like this guy."

"Come on," he pleaded. "We give this old weirdo a couple of copper pieces for the information. No harm done."

"Ugh, fine," Lerissa growled. "Here's five copper. That's all you get."

"I take the copper and walk over to our new friend," Jacob narrated. "Here you go, my friend. Now can you tell me where I might find—crap!" Jacob stopped. "What was his name?" he asked us.

"Really?" Laura groaned. "Dorn. Dorn the Bright."

"Right," Jacob mumbled. "We're looking for Dorn. Dorn the Bright. Do you know where he might be?"

"Yeah," the old man responded. "I know where he is."

"Well? Where is he?" Jake asked. Mr. R just sat there smiling with his crazy face and rubbed his fingers again.

"Okay screw this," I shouted. "I'm gonna pin him against a wall with the head of my battleaxe around his throat," I growled, slamming my fist on the table. "We gave you money already, you greedy scum! Tell us where he's at, or you're gonna lose more than the copper we gave you!" I shouted.

"Give me an intimidation roll," Mr. R told me.

"Non-natural twenty," I revealed.

"Okay, okay," Mr. R said, as the crazy man. "Dorn lives up the coast a little ways out of town. He lives there with his apprentice. Please, let me live! Let me live!" he begged.

"Are we satisfied with our answers?" I gauged the group.

"Hang on a sec," Liam spoke up. "I'm gonna take out my dagger and press it against his rib cage. Not stab, just put some pressure," he described. "Now you're going to give us our money back, apologize to our friend you tried to swindle, and then we will let you walk away with your life." Liam grabbed his die without being asked and rolled. He grew a large grin. "Natural twenty."

"Oh, yes sir, anything you ask," the man responded. "You watch him reach into his pocket and pull out a handful of money. He drops it on the ground," Mr. R narrated. "I'm sorry I tried to swindle your friend there. I really am. Now please, let me go!"

"I pull off my axe," I said. "Now scat!"

"The man runs away in fear without looking back."

"Yeah! That's right!" Jacob shouted, "Don't mess with us, boy!"

"I guess we're heading up the coast?" Lerissa asked.

"But we just got here," I whined. "Can't we go look around first? There's got to be a sailor out there willing to fight me."

"Really?" Torinn looked at me. "She has a death cult trying to kill us for being around her, we're also supposed to be inside the hidden temple of the Raven Queen tomorrow, and you want to go pick a fight in a tavern?"

"I mean yeah." I shrugged. "The heart wants what the heart wants." Torinn rolled his eyes.

"You are so dense," he told me, shaking his head.

"Fine, why don't you guys go to the wizard's house and dump all this nasty baggage out on him?" I ranted. "And I'll go find a nice brawl to go to. And since you guys don't need to take everyone to this guy's house, someone can come with me." I looked around the group to see who would join me. "Rolen?" I nudged Ben. "Old buddy, wanna go get some skull smashing fun on?"

Ben looked at me with a concerned look. "Sorry, Adrik. But Tor is right. We don't have time for picking fights. We need to figure out this whole Lerissa thing. And you're one of the people who signed that contract." Ben reached into the backpack hanging off the back of his chair. He rummaged around for a second before pulling out an accordion folder. He opened the folder and produced a brown piece of paper.

"Um, what you got there?" I asked. Ben unfolded the piece of paper and cleared his throat.

"By signing this contract, the members who sign their names on this contract, see below, agree to the following:

One, the signing party agrees to retrieve the Hammer of Oculous from the Temple of the Raven Queen located off the shores of Allurena.

Two, the signing party agrees to return the aforementioned hammer to the contract creator. See below.

Third, by signing this contract the aforementioned signing party shall be given a..." Ben stopped reading aloud.

"What's wrong?" I asked. "Why did you stop?"

"The aforementioned signing party shall be given a cursed copy of the contract that enables the aforementioned creator the ability to harm and or kill the aforementioned signing party if the first two contract clauses are not met." He looked up at me. *"Any attempt to dispel the contract's magic will result in immediate death and forfeit of all and any profits promised by the aforementioned contract creator.*

Signed Adrik Frostbeard and Rolen Naïlo."

"So, you two signed a freaking contract without reading it first?" Lerissa shouted at us. "Are you both that stupid?"

"He said it was all legal talk and stuff," I told her. "He told me it was just to ensure that he would give us our profits when we returned with the item."

"You idiots!" Ront shouted. "So not only did we think this was going to be a blind in and out sort of thing. But we could also lose both of your lives?"

"Actually, it's binding to everyone." Ben winced. "It says party. That means the whole party, not just the two who signed."

"Oh, that's just freaking awesome!" Ront moaned, throwing his hands out and looking up at the ceiling. "Are there any more surprises you all want to let us in on?"

"Oh yeah," I said. "I reach into my bag of holding and pull out my new axe from the last battle."

"What?" Ront interjected. "It's just an axe."

"Yeah, but it's more than that. It's a berserker axe. And before I attune it, I wanted to see what you all thought." I handed the item sheet to Liam.

"Is now really the best time to ask us about some weapon you have?" Liam asked grabbing the sheet.

"Well, you asked if there was anything else and I thought this qualified."

Liam drew in a deep breath. "Fine, you're right. Go ahead and attune. Not like it will matter to us when we're dead." He handed me back the sheet. "Let's just go find this Dorn guy. Maybe he can solve one of our problems."

"We start heading to.the beach and then go north up the coast," Laura said.

"You guys make your way through the busy town. The sun is now up in the sky. Maybe about mid-morning, I'd say. Walking through the town, you pass a couple of shops, and an inn. There's a tavern called the Salty Dog," Mr. R described to us.

"Oh, there!" I said, pointing. "That's where I want to go!"

"You already decided on where we were going when you signed a stupid contract," Ront let out.

"Fair," I responded hanging my head.

"You guys make your way towards the beach and pass through a local market before hitting the docks and the black sand beaches. You start making your way north along the coast line until you come to a small hut-like house," Mr. R explained.

"The second I see it I run up and knock on the door," Laura interjected. She knocked on the table.

"Hello?" Mr. R responded. His voice was feminine. Light and sweet in its greeting.

"Hello?" Lerissa responded. "I'm looking for Dorn. I was told he lived here."

"You all stand there in silence for a second," Mr. R started. "And then the door opens slowly. Eereek," he mimicked the door.

"Hello?" Lerissa asked into the door.

"The door creaks open a little wider."

"I guess I walk in." Laura shrugged.

"Are you crazy?" Liam whispered. "I'm gonna check for traps." He rolled his dice. "Eight?"

"You don't notice anything. It's just kind of dark," his uncle told him.

"Crap." Liam snapped his fingers.

"I'm gonna head in," Daryl announced.

"Are you sure?" Laura asked.

"There's only one way to find out."

"You all watch as Torinn walks through the door and disappears into the darkness," Mr. R said.

"I guess I follow in," Laura said.

"Again, the rest of you watch as she passes through into the darkness behind the door."

"Screw it! I charge in with my axe out!" I said.

"I run in with him," Jacob said.

"You both disappear into the darkness."

"Shall we then, Ront?" Ben put his hand out to Liam.

"I guess," He rolled his eyes.

"Alright you both pass into the darkness as well," Mr. R began. "As you each slip through one by one, you immediately begin falling. Further and further you feel like you're falling. But you can't see anything. It's pitch black. Like before in the forest."

"I knew it! I freaking knew there was something suspicious about this place!" Liam interrupted.

"You just keep falling further and further. No sense of where you are."

"I wanna call out to the others," Laura said. "Is anyone else here?"

"As you go to shout this, you don't hear anything. Not even your own voice as you try to speak. You feel your vocal cords move like when you speak. But nothing comes out," Mr. R described.

"Crap," Laura mumbled.

"I'm gonna cast dispel magic," Daryl announced. "Worked before. Maybe it'll work again."

"Okay, roll me a spell casting check," Mr. R said.

"Eighteen?" Daryl asked. Mr. R looked at down at something behind his screen and then returned to look at Daryl.

"All of a sudden you all hit the floor. You don't drop more than two or three feet from above it." Mr. R smiled. "What do you guys do?"

"I'm going to stand up and brush myself off," Daryl started. "And then I want to look around at where I'm at."

"Once the darkness clears, and you brush yourself off, you notice you're in a little cottage," Mr. R narrated. "There's a fire going in the fireplace, a large cauldron hanging above the fire. Every countertop is cluttered with books and parchment. Stacks of books everywhere. Some that stretch floor to ceiling. Behind you is what looks like a pantry. When you look inside, there are vials of random liquids, and herbs hanging from the ceiling. From your experience, Torinn, this is a home of a wizard." Mr. R clicked his keyboard, and the screen changed. The exact image he described presented on the screen.

"I believe we have found the place we are looking for," Torinn said.

"Hello?" Mr. R asked. He had a very aged sound to his voice. Not the one that greeted us earlier. "Who's there?"

"Hello," Daryl responded. "My name is Torinn Yarjerit. My companions and I are in search of the wizard Dorn the Bright. Would that be you?"

"You watch as a figure appears in the doorway to the next room, slightly reliant on the staff he carries. His pale purplish skin seems to be illuminated by a light behind him. His eyes are glowing white," Mr. R depicted. "What brings you to my home?"

"I do," Laura spoke up. "My name is Lerissa. I am a wizard like you. In our adventures, we have found ourselves in a predicament. During a rest in the town of Faria, we were attacked by members of Death's Hand. They are after my powers of necromancy. Madame Reita told us to seek you out in hopes you could help us."

"Reita sent you?" Mr. R asked. "Why, I haven't seen her in many years," he reminisced.

"So, can you help us then?" I asked impatiently.

"Patience my friend," Torinn calmly said.

"I might be able to help," Mr. R spoke up. "Elfi! Elfi dear, would you come down here for a second." Mr. R called behind his shoulder. "You all notice another figure come through the doorway behind the aged aasimar. A young half-elven woman appears in the doorway."

"Hold on," Ben interrupted. "Elfi the half-elf? Come on Mr. R. The book has a bunch of names you could use. Why Elfi?"

"She wasn't my creation," Mr. R responded as he held up the

character sheet to show the name at the top right. Jess. This was mom's creation.

"Really? My mom came up with the name Elfi?" I chuckled.

"I asked her if she would help me create an NPC for the game. I've been texting her all week to create Elfi," Mr. R explained.

"Gotcha," I acknowledged, snapping and shooting him some finger guns.

"Elfi, my dear," Mr. R hopped right back into character. "Come here a moment." He motioned her next to him. "Yes, sir, what is it?" He changed his voice. Reminiscent of that which greeted us at the door. "I need a little assistance," his voice changed back to Dorn's. "Up in my study, there is a tome locked away in my forbidden section. The spine reads Death's Hand. Would you retrieve this for me?" He stopped. "Right away," Mr. R responded to himself.

"A book?" I snapped. "What is a book going to help us with?"

"Are you daft?" Daryl scolded me. "You realize Lerissa uses a spell book, right? Book. B-O-O-K" he spelled out to me.

"Yeah, but that's a book with spells in it. What's a book about this cult going to do to help us?" I snarked.

Daryl slammed his hand into his forehead. "I-I can't with you," he muttered. I know that this book is probably going to help us. I'm just trying to get under his skin a little for letting me come out with lipstick on my cheek.

"Just stop it you two," Laura jumped in. "This bickering isn't going to get us anywhere!"

"Elfi returns after a couple of minutes of bickering," Mr. R stepped in. "In her hands, a large leather-bound book. On the cover, a symbol one of you recognizes," he said looking at Liam. "Ah yes, thank you, my dear," he said changing his voice into Dorn's. "He takes the tome and slams it onto the table beside him. He opens the cover and begins tracing his finger through the page." Mr. R said mimicking the actions. "Ah, here we go. The prophecy."

"I'm sorry," Lerissa chimed. "Prophecy? There wasn't anything about a prophecy."

"Oh, don't worry my child. It's not one of those you will bring balance to the world or will slay the big bad man in the end." Dorn chuckled. "This prophecy speaks of a child, abandoned by their people in a world they do not know. This child will wield unimaginable power in magic that could bring greatness to the grand army of Death's Hand."

"This can't be me," Lerissa pleaded. "I wasn't abandoned into an unknown world. I was just abandoned."

"This is ridiculous," Ront blurted out. "We've been here how long? Ten, twenty minutes? He doesn't know any of our names, and now he's reading us some random prophecy. Does none of this worry any of you?"

"I was skeptical from the beginning," I noted.

"Silence!" Dorn erupted, snapping his fingers. "Again, you both can feel your vocal cords moving as if you were talking, but nothing seems to come out."

"Thank you," Torinn said.

"Now, this prophecy speaks of many children. For instance, my apprentice, Elfi, here." Dorn motioned behind him. "She was abandoned as a child by her kingdom. I found her near my old home where I raised her and helped her hone her magic skills. Elfi is quite the powerful magic user much like yourself. Due to the vagueness of the prophecy, we are unsure of who it truly speaks of."

"Okay, now who is we?" Rolen spoke out.

"I'm sorry?" Dorn responded.

"You said *we* are unsure," Rolen emphasized. "Who is this *we* you're referring to?" he interrogated.

Dorn let out a deep sigh. "The *we* I am referring to is the Order of Corellon," he explained.

"Oh, gods, another cult?" Rolen moaned.

"We are not a cult," Dorn responded. "We are an organization of elite magic users. There are wizards like myself, warlocks, sorcerers, druids, monks, and even some bards and clerics."

"What's that supposed to mean?" Gimble and Torinn shouted simultaneously.

"I meant no disrespect," Dorn said. "But when you think of elite magic users, bards and clerics aren't usually considered."

"Save the sparing of my feelings." Gimble laughed. "I understand."

"But as I was saying, The Order is unsure of whom the prophecy speaks. That's why we all have taken on apprentices and prodigies with great power in our fields of magic." Dorn said.

"Oh, yes I'm well aware," Gimble interrupted. "And I'm going to flash him the back of my violin."

"What ya doin' there, Gimble?" Lerissa asked.

"Well, ya see, there's a bit of a secret I've been keeping from the group," he began. Jake pulled out a piece of paper from his binder and turned it towards us. On the paper was a simple crescent moon symbol. "I am one of the members of the Order of Corellon. I am the bard that he is referring to," he smiled.

"We are just full of surprises, aren't we?" Liam blurted.

"Uh, uh, uh." His uncle looked at him. "You're under a spell of silence." Liam rolled his eyes and nodded. "But my apologies for not knowing you are of the Order, master..."

"Gimble. Gimble Folkor," Jacob introduced himself. He shot his hand out towards Mr. R. "Now about this whole thing with the cult, my friend, and the prophecy."

"Ah yes," Mr. R stuttered. "Death's Hand looks to raise an army from the dead. But to do so, they need a magic user of necromancy. One powerful enough to not only create but guide a grand army across the world. Reita sent you to me I guess out of fear that you are this being."

"I'm still so confused with all of this," Lerissa jumped in. "Everyone keeps telling me they want me to raise a massive army, but I haven't been told how I stop them. Reita told me they would keep me alive so long as they need me. But how do I escape their grasp?" Laura interrogated. I'm glad she asked because I'm starting to get a bit confused too. Mr. R might have chewed off a bit more than he wanted to on this story.

"That's why you came to Allurena isn't it?" Mr. R asked. "To visit the temple and seek answers from the Raven Queen?"

"No!" She shouted. "We're here because these two," she pointed at Ben and me. "Signed a cursed contract that binds us to retrieve the Hammer of Oculous from the temple or else we all die! This whole trip has been a bigger shit-show than the time we nearly died to a tarrasque! Pardon my language." She began panting for air. We sat there for a moment in awkward silence.

"Okay," Mr. R broke the silence. "Well, here is a good solution," he said in Elfi's voice. "You're going to the temple anyways, correct? Go and speak with the Raven Queen. Get your answers from her and retrieve the item at the same time."

"And how are we supposed to speak with her? That is if she is real," Liam interjected,

"You're still under the spell, aren't you?" Mr. R asked.

"Nope," he held up his player hand book and pointed to the description of the spell. "It's been well over ten minutes since you cast the spell." He smirked at his uncle. I wasn't even paying attention to that. I would have forgotten that I was silenced had he not broken the silence before.

"Oh, thank you," I burst out. "But yeah, how are we going to meet this goddess? They don't come talk to just anyone."

"That's where you're wrong, my young adventurers," Mr. R said as Dorn. "This is where everything comes together. Tomorrow at the crack of dawn the temple will be revealed from beneath the waters of the black sand beaches of Allurena. The temple will be opened to all. But this is also when the Raven Queen revisits the temple. The temple isn't revealed just so the world may visit it. The temple is revealed for the sole purpose of the Raven Queen to physically appear in the material plane."

"So, we're going to steal a doomsday weapon from the goddess of death?" Ront questioned.

"You're a rogue aren't you?" Dorn asked.

"This is absurd!" Liam threw his hands in the air.

"Honestly though," Laura said. "What are we supposed to do? This is an absolute death wish!"

"I don't know what to tell you," Mr. R shrugged. "I can help guide you through this Death's Hand problem. But beyond that, it's your deal. I can't help you with your contract."

"Fine, whatever," Lerissa roared. "What do I need to do about Death's Hand? How do I get them off my back?"

"In the morning, you will go to the beach and watch the temple appear from the sea," Dorn instructed. "There you will make your way inside the temple and navigate into the main chamber. There you will make your claim to the Raven Queen. If your prayers are worthy, she will show herself to you and present you with the answers to your problems."

"What about the guardian of the temple?" Ront asked.

"I'm sorry?" Mr. R questioned. By his response, I guess Dorn here doesn't know everything.

"The guardian of the temple? The defender of the tomb? Reita once held these titles," he lectured. "One of the greatest warriors in the world protects the items inside the temple. You live here, shouldn't you know about this?"

"I-I've never heard of this guardian before," Dorn muttered. "Where did you learn about this?"

"The forbidden library of Tal'ireald," Liam answered. "After we were semi-forced into a contract that required us to break into a hidden temple to a goddess of death, I went and did some research. Because when a temple is hidden for most of the year, there is something in there that shouldn't be taken out. Something worth hiding."

"I would expect the same." Dorn nodded. "But why would that information be hidden away in the forbidden library?"

"That's what I would like to know," Liam agreed. "Someone is pulling a Palpatine somewhere, and I would love to know who and why." I shot a glance over at Liam and put my hand up for a high five. Star Wars reference on point!

"Are you saying that these two quests have more in common than we thought?" Jake asked.

"I think we're being played here. Think about it, some sketchy being approached the least smart members of our party." He pointed at Ben and I. I wanted to defend myself, but he wasn't wrong: Adrik is not smart, and this was half his fault. "Gets them to sign away all our lives to retrieve a doomsday weapon from the temple of the Raven Queen. And then it just happens to be the place we need to go to help rid Lerissa of this cult that's been watching her since birth? And they just suddenly decide to show up in a small town tavern in the middle of nowhere?"

"You've put a lot of thought into this whole thing," I noted. "Who do you think it is?"

"I'm not quite sure. I know for sure that our little hammer friend is behind some of this, but where he lies on the scale is beyond me." Liam rubbed his face.

"So, what do we do then?" Laura asked.

"Well personally I think we could use a real rest," Jacob

suggested. "Is there room here, Dorn? Or should we head back into town and find somewhere to stay?"

"I wish I had a place for you here," Dorn began. "But as you can see, there is barely enough room for Elfi and me. But I would be more than happy to send her with you as an escort to the Kraken Inn where you could find shelter for the night."

"That would be lovely," Ben answered hastily. "And Rolen will move towards Elfi and offer his arm."

"Subtle," Laura rolled her eyes.

"Are you sure?" Mr. R asked. "Do not worry my dear, everything will be okay," He assured himself. It's funny watching him talk to himself sometimes. But hey that's what happens when you take on the title of DM. "Alright, I guess follow me?"

"I guess we thank you for your help," Laura said.

"Ah yes, you are very welcome," Dorn nodded. "Master Frostbeard, a moment of your time before you go,"

"Yeah?" I asked.

"I want to give you this," Mr. R handed me another laminated rectangle of paper. "I want you to use this when the time is to defend and protect your party and my dear Elfi."

"Thank you..." I stopped mid-sentence. "What do you mean 'and Elfi'?"

"There is no time to explain my child. Now go! And before he sends you off, he wraps a belt around your waist, and you feel an arcane power surge through your muscles like electricity," Mr. R described.

"W-what did you just do to me?" I asked in fear.

"No time! Go!" Dorn said. "And suddenly you all are standing outside Dorn's house... with Elfi."

"So now what?" Daryl asked.

"I guess we go back to town and find a place to rest?" Jake responded.

"Guys, I don't feel right about this whole thing," I said, examining the item sheet Mr. R gave me. It read on top *Belt of Giant Strength (Fire Giant)*. Why did he give me giant's strength? And why would I have to protect Elfi? Something wasn't right here. "I feel like we're still missing a lot of information after all that."

"It's over, Addy," Torinn spoke up. "Let's just go rest up. All we need to worry about now is getting into the temple in the morning."

"I guess you're right," I sulked.

"So, you guys start heading back to town?" Mr. R asked.

"I guess so," Laura sighed.

"Let's go." Liam shrugged. Everyone seemed defeated. Like we had lost already.

"Hey, Elfi," I said to Mr. R.

"Yeah?" He responded in his female voice.

"What do you think about what just happened?"

"Well," he paused. "I don't know. You all seem to be in quite a predicament. Between a rock and a hard place. No matter what happens your outcomes seem to point towards death. But you also are a smart group of people. I can tell by how you are still alive after this long. I'm worried about the future of this group. But I'm also confident that you will succeed without dying or killing the entire world."

"That's more faith than any of us have at the moment," Ront commented. "By the looks of it, we have two options here. Die or die."

"Just ignore him, Elfi," Rolen said. "I appreciate your confidence in us."

"Do you now?" Ront asked. "Do you really? Do you not realize the situation we're in here? A situation you got us into?"

"Have you thought of any ideas beyond what these wizards keep telling us?" Rolen rebutted. "All we have been told today is death, death, death, and even more death!" His hand puppeting the words. "But have we attempted to look at it another way?

The world works in mysterious ways. In all this death talk there must be light sprouting in every corner."

"Oh, give me a break," Ront moaned. "It's always nature this and Pelor that. When will you guys see that none of these 'higher powers' actually do anything?"

"Don't you speak ill of the good Lord Pelor!" Torinn threatened.

"Or what?" Ront taunted. "What's going to happen? I have cursed the high and mighty all my life, and I haven't seen squat! If Pelor is real, why doesn't he prove it? You hear that, Pelor?" Liam shouted to the ceiling. "Prove me wrong?"

"Give me a religion roll real quick, Liam," Mr. R asked.

"Nineteen," Liam said.

8

FROM THE ASHES

"As you shout to the skies for proof, a crack of lightning spawns from the cloudless sky and strikes Dorn's house. From the distance you're at, you see the horizon begin to glow against the twilight sky," Mr. R described.

"Oh crap!" Liam's expression dropped. "I run back towards the house!"

"As you all reach closer to the house, you see flames everywhere. Where the house once stood is now a pile of rubble and flame. The entire house is reduced to nothing," Mr. R said somberly. "And when she realizes what happened, Elfi collapses to the ground in tears."

"I run up and kneel beside her, draping my cloak over her shoulders," Rolen said. Mr. R wrapped his arms around himself in a defensive position.

"Are you happy?" Torinn said to Ront.

"Y-you think I did this?" Ront responded.

"This is Pelor punishing you for cursing him!" Torinn shouted.

"You're telling me that the God of life and light killed an innocent man because I asked him to?" Ront scoffed.

"As you say this, you guys see out of the shadows, in the flames, a figure moving towards you. Elfi shouts out to the figure. Master! Master is that you?"

"I arm myself," Liam said.

"Me too," I added.

"Roll me perception checks, you two."

"Eighteen," Liam said.

"Twenty-one," I called out. This is getting really good all of a sudden. Maybe the story was meant to get all jumbled back there to throw us off.

"As you both prepare your weapons and watch the figure get closer and closer you begin to recognize the being. It's Throkk, eyes glossed over, and wounds from the last battle still present and quite fresh," Mr. R detailed.

"No way he just conjured that lightning that blew up the house," Daryl said.

"Either way, this means Death's Hand was behind it, and they're close, especially if big man is back from the dead," Liam noted.

"As Throkk gets closer you begin to hear growling come from the flames as four hellhounds make their way through the flames. Everyone roll initiative," Mr. R said.

"Fifteen," I said.

"Eight," Liam called.

"Thirteen," Jake announced.

"Fourteen," Ben claimed.

"Sixteen," Laura said. We sat there for a second in silence.

"Daryl?" Mr. R asked. "What'd you roll?" Daryl looked up in shame. He slowly raised his index finger up. "Is that a one?" Mr. R asked him. He just quietly nodded.

"Oh boy," I said.

"Lerissa, you're up first," Mr. R began.

"Great, I'm going to cast fireball," Laura called out.

"Natural one, roll some damage," Mr. R chuckled.

"Thirty-two fire damage," Laura said as she collected all her d6's again.

"Oh man," Mr. R commented. "Anything else?"

"I'm going to move over and stand in front of Elfi and Rolen," Laura directed.

"Alright, Adrik you're up."

"Good," I smiled. "First, I would like to rage. And then I'm going to take my movement and run at Throkk and use all three of my attacks on him." I grabbed my d20 and rolled it three times. "Fourteen, Natural twenty, and nineteen."

"Miss, hits, and hits," Mr. R responded.

"Twenty-five off the crit, and fifteen on the second hit." I just did some serious damage.

"Not bad," Mr. R said as he wrote the damage down. "Now it's Throkk's turn. He's going to stab at you with his spear." Mr. R rolled his die. "Ten doesn't hit you, does it?"

"Nope," I smiled.

"He's going to stab again, and that's lower than the last roll." Mr. R laughed. "Rolen." Ben sat up.

"I'm gonna cast sunbeam on Throkk," he said. "It's a seventeen constitution save for both Throkk and Adrik. Throkk has disadvantage if he's undead."

"It's a fail for Throkk," Mr. R said.

"I save with a twenty-one," I told him.

"Twenty-one radiant damage. Jack, you take eleven."

"As a beam of light bursts from the Rolen's hands and focuses on Adrik and Throkk, you feel a slight burning sensation, Adrik, as you watch Throkk burn away until he no longer exists," Mr. R depicted.

"This loser can't escape my power!" Ben laughed.

"Alright, Gimble." Mr. R turned to Jake.

"I'm gonna move over to the closest hellhound and stab him with my rapier," he said rolling his die. "Natural twenty!" He jumped throwing his hands up in the air.

"Give me damage," Mr. R sighed with a smile.

"Eleven," Jake said.

"Alright. Now it's Elfi." Mr. R began. "She's going to cast chain lightning on the other three hellhounds." Mr. R rolled a bunch of different dice behind the screen. "They all failed and took thirty-four lightning damage."

"Holy crap! Dorn wasn't kidding. She is powerful!" I blurted.

"Ront, that goes to you," Mr. R pointed to Liam.

"I'm gonna shoot my shortbow at one of the hellhounds," Liam said. "Twelve?"

"Does not hit," Mr. R shook his head.

"Ok, I'm going to move over to Gimble and end my turn."

"Okay. The three mega hurt hounds move in on Adrik in the middle of the circle. Eleven doesn't hit." Mr. R chuckles. "The other hound by Gimble and Ront is going to use fire breath. I need dexterity saving throws."

"Seventeen," Liam looked at his uncle.

"Seventeen as well." Jacob laughed.

"Alright you both take eleven fire damage." Mr. R said scanning his notes. "Torinn, you're up."

"Oh man, I'm going to run up next to Adrik and slam my mace on the first hound, twenty," Daryl looked at Mr. R.

"Hits, roll damage."

"Nine bludgeoning damage." Daryl smiles.

"Alright, you swing your mace and give a good smack at the hound sending it back a bit." Mr. R described. "The hellhound pulls back and whimpers a little bit in fear. Back to the top, Lerissa."

"I'm gonna cast fireball again." She smiled. "I'm aiming at the three hounds who are grouped together."

"Torinn, you're in the twenty-foot radius as well, so I need a dex save from you too," Mr. R said. "The hounds succeed."

"Nine," Daryl sighed.

"Well..." Laura shrugged. "Twenty-nine fire damage."

"Oh well, that's good, considering I have resistance to fire damage. I'm a freaking dragonborn." Daryl bonked his forehead with his hand.

"And it also does not affect the hounds." Mr. R chuckled. Laura's expression dropped. She was definitely not happy that she did that and didn't even think about immunities "Adrik, your turn."

"Well, I'm going to move over to Gimble and take my three attacks against the hound attacking him," I said. "Twenty-three, twenty-seven, and... natural one." I rolled my eyes. "Twenty-five slashing damage on the two that hit."

"Alright, you swing at the hound landing two blows to its face. But on the last swing, you put all your might into it, miss, and are thrown across the field into a tree." Mr. R laughed as he narrated my blunder.

"Can't have all the fun, I guess."

"Rolen, you're up," Mr. R pointed at Ben.

"I'm going to cast moonbeam on the three hounds by Torinn. But I'm going to center the beam to keep Torinn out of it," Ben described.

"They failed," Mr. R said.

"Yes!" Ben cheered. "They're gonna take..." he trailed off to roll. "Twenty-two radiant damage."

"As you focus your arcane energy at the hounds, you all watch as a bright beam of white light erupts from Rolen's hands and blasts the three hounds into oblivion." Mr. R described, flashing his fingers at us. "There is one hound left. Gimble, you're up."

"Oh man," Jake said slapping his hands together and rubbing them. "I'm going to stab at the last hound with my rapier... never mind." He sighed showing us the one on his die.

"As you go to stab at the hound, he snatches your blade in his mouth and snaps it in half," Mr. R smiled.

"You're kidding me?" Jacob complained. Mr. R just sat there and smiled. "I guess I'm just gonna disengage and move away then."

"Alright, Elfi is up. She casts a cone of cold." Mr. R began flipping through a manual. "And I need a constitution saving throw from Adrik," he pointed at me.

"Nine," I winced.

"You and the hound take forty-one cold damage," Mr. R began. "And the hound freezes solid in its tracks."

"So, it's dead?" Daryl asked.

"Yes," Mr. R nodded. "It's dead."

"Great, now can we get out of here before we all die?" I asked. "I've only got fifty-three hit points. I need some healing."

"What about Elfi?" Ben asked. "Is she able to continue on with us?"

"Give me an insight check," Mr. R responded.

"Eighteen."

"You notice that she is very distraught and in shock. Her mentor and father figure just died in a ball of fire..."

"So, she's now in the same boat as everyone at this table?" Daryl quipped. Jake gave him a menacing stare. We sat in silence for a couple of seconds.

"I'm going to walk up to her and try to comfort her," Ben interrupted the awkward silence. "A-are you okay?"

"She just shakes her head," Mr. R said calmly.

"Come on, let's get you out of here. And I help her up and

walk her towards the town," Ben narrated. Mr. R rolled a die behind his screen.

"She doesn't budge," he told Ben.

"I didn't want to do this," he complained. "I'm going to cast charm person. It's a wisdom saving throw, seventeen or higher."

"Welp," Mr. R shook his head with a smile. "She crit failed. She's all yours I guess."

"I'm just going to take her by the arm. Can I tree stride us into town near that inn?"

"Give me a nature check to see if you know any trees near the inn," Mr. R said.

"Twenty-four," Ben looked back at Mr. R.

"Yeah, I'll say you remember a couple of trees back in the town that resemble the palm trees here at the beach," Mr. R explained.

"Okay you guys, get ready," Ben said to the group. "Once the tree opens, and Elfi and I get through, hurry through! And I move Elfi and myself to the closest tree, put my hand on it and cast the spell."

"Okay. As you place your hand on the tree and focus on one of the trees back in Allurena, you began to feel an arcane energy flow from your chest, down your arm, and into the tree. As the energy escapes your body, the tree begins to open wide, and a bright light appears in the opening. Everyone steps through?" Mr. R gauged the group. We all nodded in response. 'As you each take your step through the tree, you feel a rush of air blast you in the face before you're pushed out the other side. You are all back in the town of Allurena."

"I'm going to take Elfi straight to the inn," Ben explained.

"I'm goin' with," Torinn said. "My old bones need some rest." He stood up and stretched his arms.

"I think we should all do the same," Lerissa chimed in.

"I'm gonna go shop first," I said.

"Really?" Liam asked. "You're the one who wanted to rest. You were all butt-hurt that you had less than, like, half health, which is still more than most of us have."

"I just need to get a few things, and then I'll join you guys," I explained. "Just don't sweat it okay?"

"I'm gonna follow you then," Liam told me.

"Just let me go do this okay?" I complained. I wasn't gonna shop, and he knows it. Adrik doesn't shop.

"Then I'm gonna stealth behind you, Eighteen," he announced after rolling.

"Jack, give me a perception check," Mr. R told me.

"Eighteen," I smiled at Liam.

"Both of you give me a roll off, I'll give Jack advantage though," Mr. R smiled.

"Twenty-nine!" Liam punched the air. "No way, no how can he beat that even with a nat twenty!"

"I'll concede then," I moaned rolling my eyes. "But I wanna keep my shopping a secret."

"Alright, everyone but Liam and Jack, go grab some pizza and take a little bit of a break," Mr. R said to the group. Everyone got up out of their chairs and walked back into the kitchen. Daryl ran the other way to the bathroom. And when I say ran, he ran. Kid has the tiniest bladder ever. "Okay. They're all gone, what's happening here?" Mr. R asked me.

"I want to go out away from the town and attune those items I got tonight," I explained. "The berserker axe and giant's strength belt. I'm worried you're walking us into a trap and I want to be prepared for whatever the hell you're about to throw at us!"

"How would you like to do that?" Mr. R questioned me.

"I just wanna find like a huge patch of trees and just start swinging and get it attuned," I explained to him.

"Alright, give me a quick perception check."

"Fourteen," I told him.

"It'll take you a few minutes to find a good patch of trees. You end up going back the way you came into town, and out there you find a nice little grove," he narrated to me.

"I just start swinging. Rage and all," I said.

"Okay, give me a strength check, and also an athletics check."

"You want those separate?"

"Yeah. The strength is to check how well your attacks go. The athletic is to see how long you can handle doing all of this. But because you are in rage I'll give you advantage on athletics."

"Alright, non-natural twenty for strength. And twenty-two on athletics."

"Okay, you spend the next few hours swinging and destroying trees left and right. Smashing through trees for the first two hours. But still getting a good amount of destruction after that." He stopped and took a sip from his water. "After the fifth hour of raging and destroying the trees, you begin to feel an arcane power flood from the axe into your body. This power is giving you a new feeling of rage. You recognize this energy as barbarian. You've experienced it once before in your lifetime. An uncontrollable anger. The axe is attuned." I sat and shook my head.

"I swore I would never use this power again. Not after the last time." I fiddled with the item sheet in my fingers. "What about the belt?"

"After you feel the axe's curse take hold over your body, you also feel another power resonate from the belt around your stomach. This power surges in your muscles, almost like an electric pulse through your body. And as you would go to bury your axe into the last tree for a rest, you destroy the tree. Almost to the point of obliteration," Mr. R finished narrating. "You are fully attuned to the belt as well. Your strength is now twenty-five while attuned to the belt."

"Holy crap!" I responded. I snagged the item sheet from my binder and ran over it. And like he said, twenty-five strength. This is bonkers! I'm unstoppable. But there's more to this gear than meets the eye. Dorn was very quick and adamant on shoving us out of his home quickly after we showed up. And he gave me this to protect his apprentice. Mr. R has something up his sleeve, and I'm not sure we will all make it out of this alive.

"So, are you good then?" Mr. R broke through my train of thought. "Can we bring everyone back?"

"What? Oh, yeah. I'm good," I responded. Mr. R picked up his phone off the table, and I could hear the quick typing and the swoosh of it being sent. A couple of seconds passed, and everyone began filing in behind Laura. "Adrik is going to make his way back into town and go into the inn with everyone else."

"Okay. As Adrik sets off away from the group, with Ront sneaking away behind him. You all make your way into the Kraken Inn, one of the largest buildings in Allurena. When you walk in, you are greeted by a warm lobby. Fire is crackling in the fireplace. A couple of patrons are enjoying themselves privately at the few tables that are around the lobby. But what catches your attention is the amount of light inside. Unlike the other taverns and inns you've stayed in before, this place is lit very well and is kept very nice," Mr. R described. He clicked his keyboard, and the table screen shifted into the inn lobby.

"I go straight to the counter," Laura said.

"You're greeted by a human man. How may I help you today?" Mr. R's voice dropped low and gravely.

"I need a few rooms for the night for my group here," Lerissa responded.

"What kind are ya lookin' for?" The man asked.

"What do you mean?" Lerissa looked puzzled. "Rooms are rooms aren't they?"

"Well, we've got two types here. These lower level rooms are more hostel types. Large rooms with floor mats and cots for cheap, but you share the area with others. Or upstairs we've got our nicer rooms. Individualized and private. For our more respectable patrons," he explained to Lerissa.

"Well, how much for one upstairs?" she asked.

Mr. R scratched his chin for a second before replying. "Well, a room upstairs is gonna cost you about fifty gold."

"Oh well, that's nothing. I hand him a pouch of a hundred gold and say, we'll take two."

"Right you are," The man responded. "And he reaches under the counter and pulls out two keys and hands them to you."

"I'm gonna snag one and lead Elfi upstairs," Ben said.

"I grab him by the arm. What the hell are you doing?" Laura shouted at her brother.

"I'm taking her upstairs and getting her settled," Ben responded. "Why?"

"No funny business, okay?" She glared at him.

"Oh, God! No, that's not at all what I'm doing! She's in shock! I had to charm her just to get her to leave the scene. What kind of scumbag do you take me for?" Ben looked very offended by this.

"I'm just saying. You came on to her real fast. Just wanted to make sure you're not taking advantage."

"No! I'm not. I am helping a distressed individual. She was just kicked from her home and watched what was practically her father get blown up, and then had to kill creatures to survive. I think she very well deserves a bit of help and kindness. Nothing else." Ben was red in the face.

"Okay, okay." Laura threw her hands up. "I'm sorry. I follow behind him."

"You guys head down the hall way around the corner from the counter and to the stairs. You take the stairs up and come to the second floor. Heading down the hall until you reach the two rooms you purchased. Across the hall from each other."

"I unlock the door and lead Elfi inside," Ben said.

"Alright, you walk in and see a bed and a cabinet. Not much more than that. A window across the room is the only source of light. There's a desk under the window with a half-burned candle. Besides that, not much else," Mr. R described.

"I just walk Elfi over to the bed and sit her down on the edge of the bed," Ben narrated. "And I pull up the chair from the desk and sit in front of her."

"Alright. How about the rest of you?" Mr. R looked around at the others.

"I open the other room and go inside with Torinn and Gimble I guess?" She looked at the brothers. They both nodded.

"I'm going to wander in and take out my violin and tune it. Re-hair my bow and such," Jake directed.

"Torinn just goes and lays on half the bed. Folds his hands across his chest and is out almost instantly," Daryl explained.

"I drop my staff against the wall and lay beside Tor," Laura said.

"Okay, Ben what are you up to then since they're resting," Mr. R turned to Ben.

"I wanna try and talk to Elfi. See if she knows anything," he responded. "Elfi, are you okay?"

"She just stares at the floor," Mr. R said.

"I grab her hands and ask again. Are you okay?"

"She shakes her head slowly."

"I know this is terrible. I truly do. I've lost people in my life too soon. I know the pain you're suffering, but this is not the time to close up on us. We're going to need your help here. Can you try and help me?"

"Roll me a persuasion check."

"Thirteen."

"She blinks away a tear from her eye that trails down her cheek and she speaks up, I c-can try," Mr. R muttered.

"That's all I ask for. And I reach out and wipe away her tear. Now the first thing I need to know, what did Dorn know that he wasn't sharing with us?" Mr. R rolled a die behind his screen after Ben asked.

"He…" Mr. R choked up. "He didn't share much of his private work. But he was aware of your arrival. He had been for quite some time. He knew Reita's apprentice would soon appear and be sent here."

"What do you mean? Lerissa isn't an apprentice to Reita, we barely know her," Ben asked puzzled.

"All members of the Order have apprentices. In their lifetime the member is to seek out their apprentice. Keep watch over them until they are old enough to learn and hone their talents."

"But Lerissa is well old enough and trained in her magic abilities. Reita never sought any of us out to train her."

"That's where Dorn was concerned. When Lerissa was abandoned as a child, the order told Reita she would need to take the child and raise her. But Reita didn't agree with this. Instead, she believed that to grow and become a powerful necromancer, the child would need to grow alone and fight to survive. The pain of it would grow her the way that Reita had. But then a band of druids found her and raised her."

"Yeah, my parents. They raised Lerissa when we found her in the forest," Rolen cut in.

"Reita didn't like this. The order told her that her apprentice would be lost to her in her negligence. The child would grow in the caring hands of the druids," Elfi stopped.

"No, don't stop!" Ben's voice began to grow concerned. "What happened after they told her this?"

"Reita—s-she left the order. She went after the druids," Elfi's voice began to crack a bit.

"It was a necromancer, wasn't it? I told them! I warned my parents that the undead animals attacking us were not just nature testing our bonds!" Rolen began to shout. "Why did nobody stop her?"

"They couldn't. Reita was too strong. She murdered an entire tribe of druids. Including your father Aoth, the druidic member of the Order. Master of the Western Forests."

"Wait..." Rolen choked. "Dad was a member of the Order? W-was I his apprentice?"

"I-I do not know, I'm sorry," Elfi bowed her head. "But she discovered that you had escaped with the child. And for decades, we believe she has been watching you both. Manipulating your lives until Lerissa is left to suffer and seek out her master."

"Did... did she wake that tarrasque that nearly killed us all?"

"Yes," Elfi responded under her breath. "But the Order protected you all. They have done their best to counter Reita's powers."

"So, is she the leader of Death's Hand?"

"We don't know," Elfi sighed. "The Order was not aware of this cult until very recently. But they ruled out Reita because she wished for solidarity. Dorn was not convinced she didn't have a hand in their creation. Ever since Death's Hand made themselves known, Dorn has been trying to seek out answers."

"It's all a bit too shady for my liking." I looked over to Ben and watched a tear drop from his face. This news was definitely a lot to take in.

"He was very close to figuring everything out. But then the Order had called for us. They told us that the child, Lerissa, was heading to Allurena from Faria. From Reita. They told us to prepare for the worst if they come. And you did. He knew it was only a matter of hours before Reita made it."

"He knew that Reita was going to attack, didn't he? That's why he bamfed us out of the hut before he could tell us anything." Ben began to put all the pieces together. "But this still doesn't explain who sent us this way for the Hammer. It was a human man. Not Reita." Ben sat there quiet for a bit scratching his chin in thought.

"I d-don't know what more I can tell you. This was all Dorn had shared with me before he died," Elfi said.

"Thank you, Elfi, this information was most helpful! I'm sorry for keeping you up. Please, rest. You definitely need it," Ben told Mr. R. "I'm going to leave the room and go tell the others what I learned."

"Okay. As you leave the room you are met in the hallway by Adrik followed by Ront," Mr. R began narrating.

"Where have you been?" Rolen turned and asked me.

"Like I said, shopping. What're you doing out here? It's late," I responded quickly.

"And he went with you?" Rolen asked, pointing at Ront.

"What? And Adrik turns around to see Ront behind him," I narrated.

"Liam?" Mr. R looked to his nephew.

"Yeah, I'll let them see me, why not." He shrugged and smirked at me.

"Damn it, man!" I threw my hands up.

"Anyway, come with me. I have a lot to tell you guys. And I knock on the door," Ben said.

"I'll answer the door," Jake chimed. "What?" he asked us.

"I've got major news, and you all need to hear it!" Ben responded. "And I push past Gimble and walk in."

"Alright. You walk in and see Lerissa and Torinn passed out in the one bed in the room. And a sleeping area at the foot of the bed that you assume is Gimble's." Mr. R described.

"I sit on the edge of the bed and shake the two sleeping

there," Ben said as he reached for Daryl's shoulder. "Lerissa, Tor," he whispered. "Wake up. We need to talk."

"W-what's happening" Laura stammered, faking a yawn. Good enough that I yawned.

"I proceed to explain everything Elfi and I just discussed in the other room," Ben said.

"So, you're telling me, that Reita has been behind all of this? Just because she wants me to suffer and become like her through the suffering?" Lerissa shouted. "All this crap is because of her?"

"That's what it seems like," Rolen responded calmly.

"So, then what do we do?" I interjected between the two.

"What else are we supposed to do?" Lerissa shrugged. "No matter what, if we want to live, we need to go into the temple in the morning. And if she has something to do with it..." She paused for a second. "I guess we stand and fight."

"You have my axe! And I pull out my axe and place it in the center of the group," I said, mimicking the action I described.

"And my mace," Torinn placed his hand in with mine.

"You have my daggers," Ront joined in.

"And my violin," Gimble chuckled, as he reached and added his hand to the group.

"And nature's call is with us as long as I am with you!" Rolen recited.

"Then I guess we rest up. We make for the temple first thing in the morning," Lerissa instructed.

"As you all wind down and head to your rooms and rest for the night, you all regain your health and spell slots," Mr. R said. "And the morning comes, the rising sun peers through your windows in your rooms, lighting them up."

9

MIDSUMMER

"You all begin to stir with the encroaching sunlight invading your room, what do you all do?" Mr. R asked the group.

"I'm gearing up. Preparing my spells and regaining my connection with the arcane powers of the world,' Laura explained.

"I'm going to kneel at the foot of the bed and make my prayer to Pelor," Daryl spoke up.

"And what is this prayer this time?" Mr. R asked. Daryl took in a deep breath.

"Lord Pelor, give us guidance through our adventures on this glorious day you have blessed us with. May we vanquish all these beings of evil who wish to destroy your light. Give us guidance, give us light. In Pelor we hope," Daryl prayed. He lifted his head and nodded to Mr. R.

"I'm going to kneel beside him while he prays," Liam said. Daryl grew a bit of a grin.

"I'm sharpening my axe," I joined in.

"I am fiddling out a tune," Jacob said. "Writing the song of the Friday gang." He smiled looking at the group.

"Interesting name," Mr. R chuckled. "Ben what about you?"

"I'm meditating at the foot of the bed," Ben responded. "Attuning my powers to the nature around me."

"Cool. You all take your time to do your prep. Maybe an hour or so passes by," Mr. R began. "Can I get an arcana check from all my magic users. Laura, Ben, Daryl, and Jake." They all scooped up their dice and rolled.

"Twenty-one," Laura said.

"Twenty-four," Ben added.

"Eleven," Daryl winced.

"Eight," Jake chuckled.

"Okay. Laura and Ben, you both feel a shift in the arcane presence around you. As if something has opened and is using a lot of magic to do so. Rolen, you recognize this feeling, it's one you associate with Lerissa's magic use. Just this one is more powerful," Mr. R explained.

"It's time to go, you guys," Lerissa announced.

"You all make your way down the stairs of the inn and out the lobby..." Mr. R paused. "And as you hit the streets, you're met by crowds of people in the streets. This is the celebration of Midsummer. People shouting and music is playing all around you," He clicked his keyboard, and the screen changed. He clicked it again, and music began to play. It was lively and happy jig music.

"Can we make our way to the coast?" Laura asked.

"You can," Mr. R started. "It takes a bit of pushing and shoving, but you make it to the docks area."

"Do we see the temple entrance?" Ben questioned.

"Give me a perception check," Mr. R told him.

"Fifteen?" Ben looked at Mr. R.

"Looking out at the water you don't see anything but waves crashing against the black sands," Mr. R began. "But as you're scanning the water, you notice a mirage-like wall against one of the tall cliff islands out in the distance."

"Lerissa, do you see that out there?" Ben asked his sister. She grabbed her dice and rolled it.

"Sixteen?" she asked Mr. R.

"You scan the water for a few seconds before the mirage catches your eye," Mr. R told her.

"I see it. You think that's it?" Lerissa asked Rolen.

"What else would it be? Seems kind of weird where it's at," he responded.

"How do we plan on getting out there?" I interjected

"Well, we have one of two options," Lerissa started. "We could either swim there... or get someone to take us out to it."

"Well there is no way you're getting me to swim all the way out to there," Torinn said. "So, we should maybe find someone who could get us across."

"Or..." Ben chimed. "I could cast water walk. It'll last us a whole hour, and we can just walk to it."

"What are you waiting for?" Laura asked. "Water walk us!"

"Okay, okay," Ben responded. "I cast water walk on all of us."

"I jump into the water!" I shouted.

"You splash into the water," Mr. R narrated. "But then the arcane power drags you above the surface where you stand as if it were solid ground."

"Holy crap guys! Look at me!" I laughed. "I just start running to the island."

"I climb down onto the water," Daryl said.

"I presume you all are going to get down onto the water?" Mr. R asked everyone. They nodded in response. "So, you all get down off the dock and expecting to dip into the water, you instead step on the surface, and it's as solid as ground."

"That's too freaky," Liam said.

"Are you losers coming with me or what?" I yelled at

the group.

"Guys, don't lose the dwarf again. We can't afford him to mess any of this up," Lerissa complained.

"I'll catch him," Ben sighed. "I take off after him."

"I just keep runnin' toward the island." I smiled. "Ain't no stoppin' this dwarven train!"

"Don't dwarves hate water?" Liam asked.

"Why do you think I'm running?" I shot back with an even bigger smile. "This is probably for the best. Had you guys tried to get me on a boat it would not have gone well."

"Fair point," Liam conceded.

"Okay. You guys take the next ten, twenty minutes walking against the water's current. Kind of like walking the wrong way on one of those moving sidewalks at the airport, the water is resisting your direction. But you make it across and finally land on the tiny beach of the tall rock outcropping that forms this island," Mr. R described. He clicked his keyboard, and the image shifted. He clicked again, and the room was filled with the sounds of crashing water and seagulls. "What do you guys do?"

"Is the mirage still standing?" Laura asked.

"Roll a perception check for me." Mr. R nodded.

"Fifteen?" She asked.

"You reach your hand out, and it feels like a thick watery substance that leaves your hand dry. When you place your hand on the mirage wall, you feel a bit of resistance before your hand finally passes through the air. The mirage begins to ripple." Mr. R paused. "Your arm that's half disappeared into the watery wall, begins to reappear as the wall pulls away. And before you all, a massive entrance reveals itself."

Without description, he clicked his keyboard, and the image of the island rippled away to reveal the cave entrance to the temple.

"The solid cliff wall dissipates, revealing a huge cave

entrance. Standing on each side of the entrance are massive statues of the same being. The gigantic humanoid female statues stand guard with their swords pointed down into the sand, shields before them. And on the shields is an image you've seen before; the crest of the Raven Queen. Although it looks a little different than the one you all have seen. This crest is only a raven's head. No horns." Mr. R pointed to the image.

"I pull out my axe and move in slowly," I announced.

"You sure you want to do that?" Ben asked.

"Oh right, right." I slapped my forehead. "I shove Ront in front of me and head in behind him." Liam rolled his eyes at me.

"Are you serious?" He asked me. I just shrugged at him.

"You said we need to let the rogue go in first and check for traps. And unlike our silly druid pal over there," I pointed my thumb at Ben. "I'd like to keep all my hit points as long as I can thank you very much."

"He's got you there," Ben chuckled. "You wanted to be first. So, by all means, do your thing."

"Ugh," Liam scoffed at Ben's snarky remarks. "I guess I'll check for traps." he grabbed his d20 and rolled it across the table.

"Well, you rolled a three," Jake said, handing back his dice.

"Crap!" Liam shouted. He scanned across his character sheet. "Eleven?"

"You don't notice anything, trap-wise," Mr. R started. "You see a lot of hanging vines and stalactites that protrude from the roof of the cave."

"Are we good to go?" I asked Liam.

"I guess, but let's go carefully," he responded. "Let me stay on lead..."

"I go past him and walk in," I cut Liam off.

"No, you idiot! What did I say?" Liam punched my shoulder.

"You said we were good." I smiled. "That's all Adrik heard.

What can I say? He's got selective hearing."

"We're doomed," Laura buried her face in her hands.

"Give me a dexterity saving throw, Jack," Mr. R asked me.

"And here it all goes downhill," Daryl shook his head.

"Seventeen." I folded my arms and looked away in pride.

"As Adrik makes his way into the cave and you all begin to follow, you hear the ground begin to give way and all around Adrik, the ground plummets deep into the earth. Except for the bit of solid ground beneath his feet. Adrik stands on a small bridge across a large trench," Mr. R described.

"What the hell, Ront!" I yelled at Liam. "You said it was safe!"

"And that we should proceed with caution. Clear the rocks from your ear." Ront said under his breath.

"Stop bickering and let's get moving. The faster this crap is solved, the sooner we can get onto better things," Daryl said.

"Once we get across this bridge I'm back in the lead. Clear?" Ront stared at me.

"Better keep up then," I joked. Liam didn't like that joke. The expression on his face was a dead giveaway.

"I'm going to force him towards the other end," Liam said angrily.

"Okay, okay, careful now. I don't wanna fall," I responded. I threw my hands up trying to be innocent.

"Can everyone make me a dex save to cross the bridge?" Mr. R asked.

"Twenty-five," Liam said without breaking eye contact with me.

"Twelve," Jake winced.

"Eighteen," Daryl said, letting out a long breath.

"Eighteen for me, too," Ben said, punching the air.

"Please don't mess this up," Laura said closing her eyes. She rolled her dice. "Oh, shi-"!" She caught herself quickly covering her mouth. "I'm so sorry Matt, I didn't mean to shout that."

"It's okay. Simple mistake," Mr. R said calmly. "Is it safe to guess you rolled a one?" Laura nodded in disappointment. "You all walk along the bridge one after the other. Carefully—slowly—and then Lerissa makes her way across the bridge."

"I reach out and grab her!" Liam jumped.

"And I hold him from falling behind her!" I shouted.

"I need a dex save again from Ront, and a strength check for both," Mr. R responded.

"Eighteen for my dex," Liam said before rolling again. "And nineteen strength."

"Sixteen," I added.

"You all watch as the bridge collapses beneath Lerissa's feet, just inches away from the edge. She tries to leap and catch the ledge but misses. In your reaction and haste, Ront dives in after her and gets a grip on her and Adrik, with all his might, manages to snag Ront's boots before he falls too far." Mr. R stopped to sip his water. "Like the monkeys in a barrel toy, you three dangle over a cliff edge—clinging for dear life."

"I'm gonna cast grasping vine, wrap it around starting at Addy's feet, down his arm and wrap around Ront and Lerissa to make sure they're secure. And then with the vine pull them back over the ledge to safety," Ben joined in.

"You guys feel a vine snake and wrap around you all before it finally begins to pull you three back up." Mr. R depicted.

"Thanks," Lerissa said, through panting breaths. "Guess I owe both of you my life, huh?"

"Just a little bit..." Ront started.

"Not at all," I interrupted Liam with an elbow to his ribs. "You would have done the same for us." I winked at Laura. I could feel the blood rush again into my cheeks like before. But I'm gonna play it cool. No almost dying this time. Just cool, calm, and collected.

"So, now that we've barely survived that," Daryl chimed in.

"What's the plan now?"

"We just keep going, I guess," Liam responded. "But for crying out loud, let me lead! And I press on."

"Okay. You all begin heading further into the cavern. The foliage begins to retreat the deeper you go. The torchlight along the walls begins to illuminate less and less. The musty air gets thicker and harder to breathe," Mr. R explained. The sound of the beach faded out into silence. We all sat there waiting for what was to come next. "Can you all give me a wisdom saving throw?"

"Twelve," I responded.

"Thirteen," Jacob followed.

"Natural twenty." Liam jumped. "Twenty-two total."

"Eighteen," Daryl joined in.

"Nineteen," Ben sighed in relief.

"Twelve," Laura moaned. "If I survive tonight I will be shocked.

"Okay. Liam, Daryl, Ben. Will you guys go to the kitchen real quick?" Mr. R asked. The three of them stood up and went to the kitchen. "Okay, the rest of you. As the air begins to thicken and the light starts to fade. The sounds of crashing waves and seagulls are no longer there. You all begin to lose your functionality. You begin to choke on the air that grows thicker and thicker. Your sight begins to tunnel and fade until you see stars in the dark. You try to gasp for air, but nothing fills your lungs. You all begin to feel a sensation of drowning. Your chests burn, and the pressure on your heads begins to grow painful. And just as you feel the last breaths of life escaping your bodies, you feel relief."

"Holy crap!" I interrupted gasping for air. I didn't realize how far I fell into listening. I reached into my pocket and pulled out my inhaler. I took a deep puff before giving Mr. R a thumbs up that I wasn't dying again.

"You all feel a sense of weightlessness. Floating in this dark void with no sense of direction." Mr. R paused. "And then from out of the darkness, a face as white as the moon breaks through the black nothingness. And you begin to hear a voice." He clicked his keyboard, and the face appeared in a dark background.

It was a mask, not a face. The mask had no emotion and very few features. There was a mouth and eyes with not much more. Around the mask, the darkness seemed to flutter and wave a little. I leaned up over the table to get a closer look. The darkness wasn't fluttering. They were feathers. This has to be the Raven Queen.

"Turn back now. You do not know the dangers that lie beyond this point. The path before you will only lead to destruction and death. Heed my warning, if you continue on this journey, you will be stopped. Leave now, or face your demise," the Raven Queen warned. "And then the face begins to disappear into the darkness again. You begin to suffocate again. Then you feel yourselves begin to fall. Plummeting into the black void. Then you hit the ground where you once stood. Once again regaining your ability to breathe. Jack, will you go grab the other three please?" I stood from my chair with my plate and headed back into the kitchen.

"Okay, you losers. We're done almost being murdered. Come back would ya?" I walked over to the pizza boxes and grabbed a few more slices.

"You had enough pizza?" Liam punched my shoulder.

"Oh, shut up and get back in there," I said shoving him towards the game room. We walked back in and sat down again.

"Liam, Ben, and Daryl. You three watch as the other three of your party stand frozen in their tracks. Each one's eyes were glazing over until they are white. And then seconds later the three of them collapse to the ground panting for air,' Mr. R narrated.

"A-are you guys okay?" Ront asked.

"We just... we just met her," I stammered.

"Who's her?" Torinn asked, concerned.

"The Raven Queen," Laura said, pointing at the screen. But the image was already changed. Instead of the Raven Queen, the screen was dark.

"What do you mean you met the Raven Queen?" Rolen asked. "You guys just stood there and went white-eyed for a couple of seconds."

"It was through some form of psychic magic," Gimble chimed in. "She told us to turn back. That we're going to cause death and destruction if we continue further."

"But we can't turn back!" Rolen interrupted. "Our lives are already on the line with this stupid hammer!"

"So, let's just run into death guns a-blazin' and hope that we can die at a later date?" Torinn shouted.

"What's the point of life if you don't look death in the face and tell her not today?" Gimble asked jokingly. "I say we do this, and what's the worst that happens? We die? So what? We go out gloriously; literally facing death."

"I've never been more encouraged and inspired to get myself killed.... But screw it! Let's go tell death no!" Ront cheered.

"I-I don't know guys," I broke in. "You three don't know what just happened to us. And Gimble, how are you cool with this? We just felt what her power is like. She suffocated us to the last possible moment. We go in, and she could just slaughter us." This is ridiculous! Why am I the voice of reason? Adrik should not have to explain to them the power of magic.

"You're always the one who goes in with no worries. Look at the freaking cavern behind us!" Ront shouted. "Look behind us! There is no way back from the way we came thanks to you and your recklessness. So why are you afraid now?"

"I don't want to lose any of you!" I shouted back. "I'm not

losing my family again! Not any of you! You're all in this because of me, and I've put you all at risk, and I'm afraid of losing any of you!" I could feel the tears welling in my eyes. The heat in my face.

"Do you need a second, Jack?" Mr. R asked. I realized that I was standing. I don't know how long I'd been standing for, but it definitely added to the anger I was portraying. I drew in a deep breath and closed my eyes as I sat back down.

"I-I'm okay," I shook my hand in the air. "I'm good. I let it get too personal. I'll be fine. I'm sorry."

"It's okay kiddo," Jake said. He was crouching next to me. He reached out and put his hand on my shoulder. "That's the whole point of this game. It helps us escape and weed out what's deep inside of us. Why do you think we play it during down times on base constantly?" He pulled me in for a shoulder hug. I could feel his muscles tighten when he squeezed me. "It's okay to have these moments. We all have feelings hidden in us from what happens in our lives. That's why we created this game for all of you guys. It's not just to keep you guys out of trouble. It's emotional therapy, bud." He gave me another squeeze and stood back up. "Now come on, let's escape this reality and fight death together... as a family."

I sniffed and wiped away the tears on my cheeks. "Okay, let's do this then!" I smiled.

"To death's door, we go!" Jake cheered.

"So, you all head deeper in?" Mr. R asked. We nodded silently. "You guys continue in deeper into the cave. The dim light begins to fade even more. Until you come to a giant door. The door is made from a different color stone. And on both sides of the door are the same statues from the entrance. As you approach the doors, they slowly creak open. Light floods into the cave and those of you who were taken into the Raven Queen's vision hear her whisper to you: You were warned."

10

DEATH'S DOOR

"I pull my axe back out again," I announced. "And I lead in with caution."

"Can I do my check?" Liam asked. And before his uncle could answer, he rolled his dice. "Twelve."

"You can't find any traps anywhere," Mr. R responded. "As you guys walk past the grand doors you are greeted by a wide-open temple." He clicked his keyboard, and the image appeared on the screen. "You guys stand on the upper level of the temple. Separating the lower pit-like level are large columns and three steps that wrap around the pit. And in the middle of the pit lays a massive hammer buried in a gigantic rock protruding from the ground."

"I'm going to move into the pit and slowly make my way to the hammer," I said.

"Adrik, wait," Torinn said. "Let me go first."

"What are you doing?" I whispered angrily as he pushed past me before I can stop him.

"I am a servant of the Lord Pelor. That may help us in not being murdered," Torinn responded as he made his way down into the pit.

"As you step into the sandy floor of the pit, you all hear a blood-curdling scream echo through the chamber. And an explosion of shadows smashes into the ground between you all and the hammer. Emerging from the shadows is a creature of light. As the humanoid breaks through the dark shadows, you notice a pale purple-skinned aasimar. Much like Dorn, but instead of the glowing white eyes, this aasimar has black misty shadow-eyes. Her black plate armor with a white Raven Queen insignia contrasts against the bright wings of light that sprout from her back. She rises from her kneeling position and looks to you all." Mr. R clicked the keyboard again, and the image of the temple added the aasimar image in the middle of the pit. "She speaks out to you all in a booming, echoing voice... You were warned. Turn back now, or you will all perish by the Raven Queen's hand!"

"I'm going to slowly step forward, shield and mace down. My name is Torinn Yarjerit, I, too, am a guardian of faith. We do not come seeking any confrontation with you or your goddess. We have come to find we are tied up in a conspiracy larger than ourselves. To find any solution to this, we require the item you are charged with defending. We ask you and your goddess to please help us," Torinn finished as he tightly grasped his holy symbol on his chest.

Mr. R glared at him. "You come to retrieve an item of destruction from the goddess of death herself. To release it into the world of man. You are fools and will be quickly dealt with," Mr. R boomed. "And she stretches her hand and blasts you with sacred flame..."

"I cast guardian of faith in front of me," Daryl interrupted.

"As you all watch the aasimar blast Torinn with fire, you see a large being of arcane energy stand in front of him holding a shield out above Torinn, defending him from the blast of flame," Mr. R narrated. "As the flames dissipate around the arcane being, the aasimar moves her hands together in front of her, and you watch as a great sword forms out of shadows into her hands. She begins running at Torinn with the sword high above her head. I need everyone to roll initiative," Mr. R said. We all grabbed our d20's and rolled them.

"Sixteen," Daryl announced.

"Six," I groaned.

"Seventeen," Laura added.

"Thirteen," Jake joined.

"Seven," Ben added.

"Thirteen," Liam finished.

"Laura take the first action." Mr. R turned.

"I cast Evard's black tentacles. It's a dexterity save of sixteen," Laura directed.

"Well that comes out to be a one," Mr. R laughed. "What happens?"

"As she runs at Torinn, black slimy tentacles erupt from the ground beneath her and restrain her. She also takes..." Laura took a handful of dice and rolled them. "Fifteen bludgeoning damage."

"Alright. You all watch tentacles appear from the ground, stopping the guardian in her tracks, lifting her up off her feet."

"I want to tell her. We're not here to fight!" Daryl jumped in. "Please don't make us do this!"

"Well, that was quicker than I thought it was going to be," Mr. R said in a familiar voice. "And you all turn to see Madame Reita walking through the doorway."

"I turn my axe at her," I growled. "What are you doing here?"

"Oh, silly child," Mr. R chuckled. "And she waves her hand in the air, shooing you to the right. Make me a strength check."

"Twenty-one," I snarled.

"You feel an invisible arcane power than knocks you over. It doesn't blow you away, but it knocks you off your feet." Mr. R explained.

"Don't move any further!" Ben shouted. "And I aim my hands up at her."

"And what are you going to do, young druid?" Mr. R scoffed. "Your father couldn't stop me. Your mother had no power against me. What makes you think you're any different?"

"Don't test me," Rolen growled.

"What do you want, Reita?" Ront joined in on the interrogation.

"You already know what I want." Reita smiled. "I've come to destroy this temple! And sever the Raven Queen's only tie to this world!"

"What are you talking about?" Ront barked.

"You spent all that time researching, and you didn't learn the temple's sole purpose?" Reita chuckled.

"To hide the Hammer of Oculous from people like you!" Ront glared at Reita. "To make sure psychopaths like you don't get their grubby hands on the fate of the world!"

"Ignorant child," Reita snapped back. "You know nothing, do you? That hammer isn't just a holding place for Oculous' soul. It's the Raven Queen's anchor to this world. Without it, in this temple, she no longer has the power to control death in this world."

"What does that have to do with you?" I shouted. "And I'm going to get back on my feet and move between her and the rest of the party."

"Power. I seek the power she has taken from beings like myself. Like you... Lerissa. And she looks right at you," Mr. R said, pointing at Laura.

"What do you mean?" Lerissa asked.

"You feel it constantly I know it. With every death around the world, you and I grow stronger. You know the feeling I'm talking about." Reita's smile began to fade. "But she robs us of this power! Taking the souls from our world for her own personal gain! And now we stand here, in the hidden temple. And I can finally destroy her once and for all!"

"And you think we're just going to step aside and let you just take all this power?" Ront laughed.

"They might not." Mr. R smiled again. "But you will. Make me a constitution saving throw."

"Fourteen," Liam snarled.

"As she says this, you begin to feel your arm burn. You begin losing your free will and can feel your entire body resist your thoughts," Mr. R said.

"Oh God," Liam said, shocked.

"Stop it!" Lerissa shouted. "Let him go!"

"Then help me, child!" Reita grinned. "Take back the power that belongs to us."

I suddenly pulled out my sticky notes and began writing a note. Once I finished it, I folded it and slid it to Mr. R without anyone seeing.

"Fine!" Lerissa shouted at Reita. "Let him go and I will help you."

"Oh, my child, I'm so glad to hear that." Mr. R smirked. "Liam make another constitution check."

"Natural twenty," Liam smirked, folding his arms across his chest.

"You begin to feel the slow regain of control of your body," Mr. R said. "But your arm still burns." Mr. R picked up the note and read it behind his screen. He grabbed his pencil and began writing on the sticky note before passing it back to me with another slip of paper with it. It's the item card for the hammer. "As you all continue your stammering and pleading for life, the tentacles drop and release the guardian," Mr. R narrated. "Torinn, it is your turn in combat."

"I'm going to move my guardian of faith in front of the guardian of the temple," Daryl started. "And then I take my movement to move to the others, stand my ground against Reita, and I'm going to fire-breath Reita. Dexterity save of thirteen."

"Saves," Mr. R responded. Daryl went through his dice box and carefully pulled out three d6's. He rolled them.

"Then she takes five fire damage," Daryl groaned.

"Alright. Jake, you're up." Mr. R turned to Jacob.

"I'm going to use polymorph on myself and turn myself into a winter wolf," Jake narrated. "And then move myself between the group and Reita."

"And making its way past you all is a snarling white wolf with a violin strapped to its back. It positions itself in front of you all," Mr. R described. "Ront, you wanna roll another con check?"

"Fifteen," Liam looked at his uncle.

"You finally feel the release of the spell over your body, and you regain control. What do you do?" Mr. R asked.

"I want to stealth away from the fight and try to move behind Reita," Liam explained. "Twenty-three."

"You manage to disappear from view, sneaking behind Reita in the shadows," Mr. R narrated. "And the guardian continues her attack. She moves up at the arcane guardian Torinn created..."

"If she gets within ten feet of the guardian she takes ten radiant damage," Daryl noted.

"She steps to swing at the guardian, winces at the pain, but takes a swing at the guardian's shield." Mr. R rolled some dice behind the screen. "Her sword bounces off the arcane shield. She swings a second time—and it ricochets off the shield again. Rolen, your move." He gestured to Ben.

"Psh," Ben sighed. "I'm going to use my two wild shapes and become an earth elemental." And Ben jumped up from his chair and walked over to Mr. R's miniature shelf and grabbed the rock creature and placed it next to his mini in front of him.

"Where once stood your half-elf friend, now stands a large rock creature that towers over everyone and displaces one of the columns," Mr. R said.

"And then I'll move and stand behind and over wolf Gimble," Ben narrated.

"You all feel the ground shake and rumble as the elemental move into his position. Adrik, your turn." Mr. R said turning to me.

"I am going to move to the hammer. Pull out the berserker axe in one hand, reach out with the other, and grab the hammer," I announced.

"Adrik suddenly retreats from the front of the group and walks to the center of the temple as you all prepare your defenses. And as the dwarf makes contact with the hammer's massive handle..." Mr. R paused. "The temple begins to rumble and shake. As everything is going insane, Adrik begins to grow, and grow, and grow!" Mr. R clicked his keyboard and in fades an image of a fire giant holding a massive war-hammer.

"Enough of this pettiness!" I bellowed. "I am... Oculous!" I shook my hands in the air. "And I want to move towards everyone and smash Reita and avoid the group."

"I need an attack roll from you," Mr. R said pointing at me. "And a dexterity save from the rest of you," He finished scanning his finger across the rest of the table.

"Twenty-six to hit," I responded.

"Since I'm hidden away, do I need a roll?" Liam asked.

"I'm going to say yes," his uncle responded. "Make sure that you won't get hit by the hammer."

"Sixteen then," Liam answered.

"Seven," Laura groaned.

"Fifteen," Daryl added.

"Nat twenty," Jake smirked leaning back into his chair.

"Five," Ben laughed. "I guess it was coming. Giant rock monsters don't move quickly."

"You all watch as the giant that was once the small dwarf you love, swings his massive hammer above you and brings it crashing down on top of Reita," Mr. R revealed.

"You're kidding me, right?" Laura interjected. "That can't seriously have been how it ends!"

"Well since you and your brother failed your dex saves, let Jack tell you how much damage you took," Mr. R responded with a smirk. I didn't think about damage. I picked up the item card for the hammer, and it read

3d6 +7 bludgeoning damage. Thunderwave: When smashed into a surface, all players in a thirty-foot radius of the hammer's contact point must make a dexterity saving throw. On a failed save players take 2d8 thunder damage. Or half on a successful save.

I probably should've read the card first before smashing it around. "Well, crap…" I chuckled. I sifted through my dice bag and pulled out three d6's and my two d8's. I rolled… And I could feel my face grow concerned. "Well, the initial attack is only fifteen bludgeoning damage." I rolled my d8's. Not any better. "And five thunder damage, ugh!" I grunted.

"Ben, I need a concentration check on your elemental form," Mr. R said without looking up from behind his screen.

"Ten," Ben said. His face scrunched.

"You hold the concentration on your wild shape." Mr. R responded.

"So now what?" Daryl interjected.

"Well, give me a perception check." Mr. R smiled back.

"Nine," Daryl sighed.

"Well, you don't notice anything new," Mr. R said. His tone seemed dry. Like he wasn't noting something… Oh shit!

"The guardian!" I shouted in my heavy giant voice.

"And as you all hear the massive fire giant shout that, the guardian charges at you all!" Mr. R rushed. "She sticks her hand out aimed at you all and blasts sacred flame at Torinn."

"What?" Daryl shouted. "Why me?"

"You are the one who approached her first," Mr. R beamed. He was a devious DM. I'll give him that. "I need a dexterity saving throw."

"Thirteen?" Daryl looked up.

"Just saves," Mr. R said. "You take sixteen fire damage, halved," Daryl mumbled under his breath as he changed his current hit points. I couldn't make out much of it. But I'm pretty sure the majority of it was swearing. "Lerissa, we're back to you again."

"Oh, crap..." Laura snapped back into reality. She began flipping through her binder. "Umm." She hummed. She started clicking her tongue in thought.

"The guardian begins charging closer to Torinn. Her sword swung back," Mr. R pressured.

"Ahh!" Laura screamed. "I cast lightning bolt at her!"

"Okay, what's her save?" He asked her.

"Dexterity," Laura said calming down. "Needs to beat a sixteen." Mr. R rolled behind his screen. With a loud thud against the wood edging behind his screen, he looked back up at Laura.

"Seventeen." He chuckled. Laura scoffed and rolled a bunch of damage dice.

"Then she takes..." She trailed off calculating with her finger in the air. "Thirty-seven lightning damage halved." Mr. R ducked behind his screen again and wrote down what I presume was the damage.

"Torinn, your turn." Mr. R pointed to Daryl over the screen with his pencil without looking up.

"I guess we're attacking now?" Daryl asked, looking at Laura.

"I don't know, what do you wanna do?" Laura snapped defensively.

"I'm going to charge at her with my shield and attack with my mace," Daryl said. His face looked slightly confused. Almost like he didn't know why he was doing that.

"Roll an attack," Mr. R responded.

"Eighteen," Daryl said. Mr. R nodded to him, letting him know he hit. Daryl rolled his damage. "Five bludgeoning damage."

"You all watch as Torinn, who is usually slow and takes his time, is in a full force charge towards the aasimar. His shield held in front, mace dragging behind him," Mr. R narrated excitedly. "As the two clashed, Torinn knocked away the guardian's own mace. And then with a huge crack, Torinn smashed his mace across the guardian's face, knocking her back off her feet." Daryl sat back in his seat and smiled crossing his arms.

"Catch." He snickered. "Who's next?"

"Gimble," Mr. R responded. And like usual, Jake clapped his hands together and gave them a rub.

"I'm going to give a massive howl... and then charge at the guardian and give her a nice bit of frost bite." He smiled. "She needs to make a dex save of twelve."

"It's a fail," Mr. R said picking his head back up.

"She takes eighteen cold damage." Jake laughed.

"After a nice crack in the face from Torinn, she then gets attacked by the large snow white wolf. As the wolf opens its mouth as if to howl, a white cloud mists out with power and a thick layer of ice begins to grow out of the mist on the guardian's chest," Mr. R described.

"That bites," Jacob laughed again. Mr. R began writing behind his screen.

"Ront," Mr. R said looking back up towards his nephew.

"Am I still hidden away?" Liam asked.

"I'll say yes since you never came out of it yet," Mr. R contemplated aloud.

"Okay, I want to sneak around and flank the guardian at a distance. And then take a shot with my shortbow," Liam said. "I have sneak attack since I'm using stealth right?" He questioned. His uncle nodded. "Cool, twenty-three to hit?" He asked.

"Hits," Mr. R responded. Liam grabbed a handful of d6's and rolled them. He grouped them back together and counted them in his head.

"Thirty-one piercing damage." Liam grinned.

"And after being mostly frozen, an arrow flies out of nowhere and buries itself into her unfrozen side," Mr. R narrated. "Argh!" He shouted. "You fools! You have killed us all! As she shouts this at you all, you watch her eyes begin to mist more with shadow than before. Suddenly blood red pupils appear out of the misty shadows of her eyes, and the aasimar begins shouting in a language that sounds like demonic gibberish to you all," Mr. R said. "Morah sarash tokoour matae keatook! Ren'aunt tearmoour voodrwar mataeka soonrar!" Mr. R began growling. "And you all watch as the guardian's body bursts into a shadowy mist."

"What the hell just happened?" Liam interjected.

"Rolen, it's your turn," Mr. R said ignoring his nephew's question.

"Wait, what?" Ben stammered to ask. "W-we're out of combat, aren't we? There's no one left to fight."

"Well it's your turn," Mr. R persisted.

"I-I guess I drop my elemental form?" Ben said, his face confused.

"And the giant rock monster began to shrink back into the half-elf druid," Mr. R described.

"That... ends my turn?" Ben said even more confused.

"Oculous, your turn." Mr. R said turning to me. "I need a wisdom saving throw from you."

I grabbed my die and rolled. "Ten?" I looked at Ben, sharing the same confused look.

"You feel an encroaching arcane power growing inside your head. Like vines creeping from the back of your brain and making their way from the base of your skull," Mr. R described. He was mimicking the feeling with his hands. Extending his fingers and making them crawl along the imaginary skull in his hands. "You hear a deep voice inside your head, it speaks to you. Thank you for freeing me, foolish mortal! Now I may once more conquer this world in the name of Oculous!" Mr. R boomed.

"Do I still have control?" I asked.

"You do, but you can feel his power growing stronger. He is taking back his form," Mr. R responded.

"I want to shout, Guys! We have a problem!" I shouted to the group.

"You all feel the booming voice of Adrik come from the massive fire giant shouting that," Mr. R said.

"Don't say that." Liam moaned.

"I'm losing control of this form! He's trying to come back!" I shouted again.

"What? Who is?" Laura shouted.

"Mrs. Butterworth! Who do you think?" I snapped back sarcastically. "It's Oculous!"

"Make me another wisdom saving throw," Mr. R interjected.

"Seven." I winced.

"You feel your muscles begin to lift the hammer from its crater, even though you're not doing that," Mr. R described.

"Guys! You'd better run!" I shouted.

11

IRONIC, ISN'T IT?

"The fire giant lifted his hammer high over his head and moved towards the two standing over where the guardian's body once laid. I need a dexterity save from you both, and a constitution save from everyone," Mr. R requested.

"Great!" Liam rolled his eyes.

"Seventeen for my dex save," Daryl said. "And fifteen constitution."

"Ten dex, thirteen con," Jake joined.

"Sixteen," Liam added.

"Fifteen," Laura said.

"Thirteen," Ben offered as he cringed.

"You both jump from the hammer's impact. Everyone takes six thunder damage halved," Mr. R said looking up from his screen. "The giant moves to lift his hammer back up. Jack make me another wisdom check."

I rolled my dice again. "Four," I whined.

"He lifted the hammer up again and repositioned it to smash you both again. Everyone save again."

"Good lord," Daryl commented. "Thirteen dexterity. Fourteen constitution."

"Seventeen dex. Ten con," Jake said.

"Come on, man," Liam moaned. "Fourteen." He shook his head at me. I shrugged.

"Six," Ben cringed again.

"Five," Laura groaned.

"You both jump away from the hammer again," Mr. R started. "And you all take fourteen thunder damage. Halved for everyone but Laura and Ben," he said.

"Damn it!" Laura blurted out. She began writing her damage onto her sheet.

"Lerissa, you're up," Mr. R pointed to Laura.

"At this point, I'm going to start running away," Laura said. "I'm going to run for the doors."

"Alright," Mr. R said. "You turn away from all your friends and the combat and make your way to the doors. But as you approach the doors, a familiar black mist begins to form in the doorway, taking on a humanoid shape."

"Son of a-" Laura stopped herself.

"The mist begins to fill out," Mr. R began. "And out of the mist walks Madame Reita." He smirked. It was that smirk that you could tell ate at Laura's soul.

"God bless it!" She complained. "I pull out my spell book, and cast conjure elemental. I'm going to create a fire elemental."

"As you stop in your tracks and pull out your book. You read the words to cast the spell. The lettering on the page begins to glow bright white, and in front of you a swirl of flame in the shape of a humanoid," Mr. R said. He turned around and grabbed a mini off the shelf behind him. He set it on the table in front of Laura. It was a fiery figure that stood a bit larger than the Lerissa's mini. "Torinn, you're up again."

"Is there any water in the cavern at all?" Daryl asked.

"There is very little water in the temple. Most of it is from the little cracks in the ceiling. Just small drops," Mr. R explained.

"That's all I need," Daryl said. He clapped his hands together and rubbed them like his brother. "I'm going to cast control water. I want to redirect flow from the ocean above through the cracks in the ceiling and splash over Oculous." Daryl grinned.

"Alright. You all begin to hear the rushing of water. Suddenly that rushing water crashes through the ceiling. Splashing down on top of the giant. Encasing him in a cube of water," Mr. R described. "Gimble?" he turned back to Jacob.

"I'm going to move on Oculous and give him a little bit of cold breath," Jake said, shooting me finger guns.

"Well, I rolled an eight..." I said with a bit of relief.

"He takes eighteen cold damage then," Jake smiled. He blew on his finger guns and pretended to holster them in his sides.

"From the wolf's snout, the familiar cloud bursts against the giant's leg. Encasing the ankle in ice. You will take thirty-six cold damage. On account of being a fire giant," he emphasized. "Ragh!" Mr. R growled. "I shall take great pleasure in burying you all beneath the rubble of this forsaken temple!" He howled. His arms stretched out from his sides. "Roll another wisdom save." Mr. R pointed at me.

"Seven," I groaned. These rolls are not going too well for me all of a sudden.

"You still manage to hang in there. But you're are fighting a losing battle, my friend," he told me. "Ront, your turn."

Liam clicked his tongue in thought. "I'm going to shift positions and shoot another arrow off at Oculous." He rolled his dice. "Twenty-three?"

"Hits," his uncle responded.

"Still sneak attack," Liam muttered as he gathered his dice. "Thirty-two piercing."

"An arrow flies out of the shadows again, this time landing

on the side of the giant's thick neck," Mr. R said before looking back down to write on his page. "Rolen?"

Ben snapped to attention after fiddling with his d20. "Oh um, well crap," he stumbled. "Should have stayed in my elemental form," he muttered to himself. "I'll cast ice storm around Oculous. Dex save of seventeen."

"It's a big fat fail," Mr. R responded. Ben grabbed a handful of dice and rolled them.

"Nine cold damage and eight bludgeoning," Ben counted. "Seventeen total."

"You all watch a cloud begin to form above the giant's head before dropping thick chunks of hail against him, pelting his thick skin," Mr. R described. "He lets out another huge roar of pain. Give me another wisdom save, Jack." I rolled again, praying to get rid of this crap!

"Fifteen!" I shouted. This was probably the most exciting thing of the night!

"Like thawing ice, you feel your mental power fight back against the arcane power that was growing in your head," Mr. R said miming the action with his hands.

"Guys! I'm trying to stop him!" I let out.

"We're screwed anyway," Laura responded. She wasn't totally wrong. But wasn't completely right either. We've been through worse.

"Adrik, you suddenly feel your entire body seize up," Mr. R continued. "And with a massive crash that shakes the ground, and you all see the fire giant frozen on the ground, stunned."

"But I'm still a giant?" I asked.

"Wanna see?" he responded. I took my d20 and rolled it.

"Eighteen?" I said.

"And the stunned giant begins to shrink back into the stocky dwarf it once was." Mr. R smiled.

"Oh my god! Thank you!" I blurted.

"That power... It shall be mine!" Mr. R shouted, clenching his fist like Darth Vader. "And we round up back to the top of the order to Laura."

"I'm gonna cast fireball at her," Laura said, sifting through her binder.

Mr. R rolled behind his screen. "No, save."

Laura snagged her d6's and rolled them. "She takes forty-one fire damage."

"You aim your hands at Reita and a ball of fire blasts at her, throwing her back towards the doorway," Mr. R described.

"And then I wanna move my elemental towards her and have it give her a nice double smack." Laura giggled. "Eleven and fifteen to hit?"

"Both hits," Mr. R responded.

"Seven on the first hit," Laura rolled again. "And eleven on the second hit."

"The fire elemental shuffles over to Reita and smacks her once, followed by a second slap that singes her face," Mr. R started. "After the second slap, she collapses to the ground. You fools!" Mr. R said. He brushed his wrist against his lower lip as if to wipe away the blood. "Do you have any idea the powers you are throwing away? With that hammer, and our combined powers," He motioned to Laura and himself. "We could rule the world!"

"You pathetic little weasel," Laura scowled. "And why would we let someone like you keep that kind of power? After all you have done to us? Leaving me to suffer as a child, murdering Rolen's tribe! His parents!"

"Torinn, your turn," Mr. R interrupted.

"You know, I'm gonna skip my turn." Daryl smiled. "I believe there is someone else in our group who deserves this more than I do. And by the way, she's pleading, I think she's very close to death."

"Gimble?" Mr. R asked Jake.

"I think I'll leave her for Rolen," Jake responded.

"Ront?" He turned to his nephew.

"Would you like to do the honors, my friend?" Liam turned to Ben.

"You know, as much as I want vengeance for my tribe and also my parents, as a druid, I am a preserver of all life. I think Lerissa deserves vengeance anyways." Ben responded to the offer.

"I agree," I joined. Ben gave me a side-eye smile. I could hear him saying, of course, you do.

"I guess that's that. Laura, what do you want to do?" Mr. R asked.

"I guess…" Laura clicked her tongue. "I'm gonna walk up to her, place my hand on her shoulder, bend down to her face and whisper to her. You will never taste such power. And I cast chill touch." Laura smirked. "This is for the Naïlos."

"Everyone but Laura give me a perception check," Mr. R said.

"Natural one," I sighed.

"Ten?" Jake asked.

"Five," Daryl rolled his eyes.

"Eight," Ben groaned.

"Twenty-one," Liam said shocked. "You guys okay there?"

"Ront, you notice as Lerissa's hand begins to grow black from necrotic powers at her fingertips. In Reita's hand, shadows begin to swarm and fill her hand and form a dagger in her fist." Mr. R described.

"Lerissa! No!" Liam shouted. "And I use all my movement and dash to push her out of the way."

"As Lerissa begins to cast chill touch, Ront barrels his way at her and shoves her out of the way just before Reita could stab her. But buried in the stomach of the half-orc rogue is a black dagger misting with shadows. You feel all the life inside of you being drained as you begin to grow cold." Mr. R said.

"Ironic, isn't it Reita?" Ront smiled.

"She looks at you confused and disgusted," Mr. R said. His expression matched that which he explained.

"That I'm the one who doesn't believe in these gods, and I'll be the second one to meet them. And then with the last bit of life I have, I stab her with my dagger." Liam grinned.

"Roll to hit," his uncle responded.

Liam rolled his die. He looked back up with a huge smile. "Natural... twenty," and without being asked Liam rolled his d4. "Does this get sneak attack damage as well?" he asked.

"Yeah," Mr. R responded quickly.

"Twenty-eight piercing damage," Liam said brushing off his lip as his uncle did earlier. "Yippy ki-yay, mother trucker "

"And with his last breaths of life, Ront buries his dagger deep into Reita's chest. She lets out a blood-curdling screech," Mr. R said. "You fools! And with her last words, Reita bursts into shadows."

"I run over to Ront and hold his head in my lap," Laura interjected. "Are you insane?" she asked Liam.

"O-only on Fridays," Liam smiled. He chuckled and then began coughing. "I guess I finally get to meet those gods you all worship." He laughed.

"No, you can't die on me now!" Daryl said. "I won't allow it! I want to cast revivify on my dying friend."

"As you cast the spell, you feel the warm arcane energy move from your hand into Ront's body—and nothing happens." Mr. R described.

"Stupid," Daryl smacked his forehead. "Dying, not dead." He shook his head.

"It's okay bud, there's no need to worry," Ront said softly. "Sometimes we all must let go."

"Hey, psycho." Ben punched Liam's shoulder. "If you must go, tell my parents I miss them, and Lerissa and I are doing great."

"W-will do buddy." Ront smiled.

"And with the last request, Ront's last and final breath escapes his lips. His body goes limp in Lerissa's lap and finally goes cold," Mr. R said softly.

"Now cracks a noble heart. Good night sweet prince and flights of angels sing thee to thy rest," Gimble recited. "And I pull out my violin and play softly in the wake of his death."

"Liam, roll me a wisdom check," Mr. R asked.

"Twenty-one," he responded.

"Alright. Ront," Mr. R turned to Liam. "As life fades into darkness, you find yourself in a state of nothingness. weightless, blackness, nothing."

"I called it!" Liam laughed.

12

FLIGHTS OF ANGELS

"And then out of the darkness, a white face appears out of the nothing," Mr. R explained.

"So, is this death?" Liam asked.

"This, my child," Mr. R began. "This is judgment."

"Judgment?" Liam asked.

"This state of limbo, this is where we decide your fate," Mr. R explained. He clicked his keyboard and on the screen returned the familiar face of the Raven Queen's mask. "This is where we decide whether those who have passed beyond their lives deserve a second chance."

"Who is 'we'?" Liam questioned.

Mr. R clicked his keyboard again, and another image appeared next to the Raven Queen. An image was of another woman. This woman had a bright yellow glow with long blonde hair. Her face wore a smile instead of the expressionless face of the Raven Queen's mask. "We are we," Mr. R said. "I am Pelor. This is my sister. We are life and death, yin and yang, good and evil. We are the cosmos and all of the planes. We create and destroy life as we see fit. And this, my young friend, is why you have come before us."

"So, what do I have to do here? Prove myself worthy of a second chance at life?" Liam questioned.

"No," Mr. R responded. "You have already proven yourself in your valiant death, sacrificing yourself to save another. But to get your second life, we ask for more from you in your life."

"Well, what do you want from me?" Liam asked.

"We ask for your servitude in this next life. As a champion for us," the Raven Queen said. "And as you have a companion already who serves my sister, Pelor," he paused. "You shall become a servant of my domain."

"You're kidding me?" Ront blurted. "I have spent my entire life renouncing the both of you. And for mostly good reasons. And now you want me to serve you?" Liam began laughing. A rumbling laugh from deep in his gut. He almost fell over out of his chair. "Alright, I'll bite," He smiled as he cupped his hands over his mouth. "What is thy bidding... my master."

I almost fell out of my chair after that one. For being dead, Liam is taking this really well.

"In your next life, you shall serve as a paladin under my domain. And with one sole purpose—to rid the world of the evil that is Death's Hand," Mr. R said.

"Wait, I thought Reita was Death's Hand?" Liam interrupted. "And I thought they worshipped you. Why destroy them?"

"Death's Hand is much larger than you know, my child. Reita was merely a pawn in their scheme for domination," Mr. R answered. "This group believes to hold to the core values of my faith. But they have grown out of control; become radicalized. And that is why you, Ront, must be my hand in bringing an end to their tyranny and treachery. If we give you life once more, you and your dragonborn friend must bring an end to Death's Hand once and for all."

"You want me and grandpa back there to destroy a group of genocidal freaks?" Liam asked.

"Yes, my child," Mr. R whispered.

"Screw it, why the hell not?" Liam shrugged.

"Then go, my champion," Mr. R said softly. "And out of the darkness, a pale white hand reaches out and extends a finger. You feel the icy cold touch of the Raven Queen's finger on your forehead. You feel yourself fall back into your body. With a gasp for air, you choke back into life. Laying there in the hands of your friends... I mean your family," Mr. R said with a smile.

"Oh, thank god!" I blurted out. "I'm gonna wring his neck with a tight hug."

"Ack!" Liam pretend choked. "You're suffocating me!"

"Good! Don't ever die again!" I scolded him.

"Glad to see you, too." He chuckled. He shifted to face Torinn. "We have a situation of major concern."

"Oh boy." Torinn smiled. "Does this mean what I think it means?"

"Almost," Ront said, rubbing the back of his neck. "I met your god. She is part of why I'm back..."

"Pelor is a she!?" Torinn interrupted.

"I guess so, both her and the Raven Queen are sisters." Ront smiled. "And they left me in a place of judgment. And left me with a choice. Either I could remain dead, or return to the world with one condition..."

"Well spit it out, what did you do? Sell your soul to death herself?" I blurted.

"Yes." He side-eyed me.

"Wait, you were brought back by Pelor, God... Goddess of light and life? To serve her polar opposite? The goddess of death?" Torinn asked, confused.

"Yeah, and it's your fault." Ront pointed at Torinn. "I was chosen to be the new champion of the Raven Queen because my companion was already a champion of Pelor."

"Why does it matter if I am already one? Why not have two?" Torinn wondered.

"Balance I think," Ront responded. "Yin and Yang sort of thing. But who cares? That's not the important part!" He shook his head regaining his thoughts. "Pelor and The Raven Queen have given us a mission. A purpose."

"You're taking orders from somebody you didn't believe in for how long? And now all of a sudden it's like it never happened?" Lerissa asked.

"Stop changing the subject against me!" Ront groaned. "Death's Hand is still around..."

"I thought Reita was Death's Hand?" Lerissa interrupted.

"Apparently, she was a small pawn in their large scheme," Ront answered. "And we've been..." He flashed his finger between Torinn and himself. "Given the lovely task of destroying them."

"Oh, you've got to be kidding me!" Rolen spoke up. "You are murdered by some crazy powerful wizard lady, and now we're being sent on a suicide mission to take down an even more powerful being?" He looked around the group. "Anybody else kind of concerned about the fact this is definite suicide? Addy? Tor? Gimble?"

"We were locked into this before we even knew about it." I shrugged.

"I mean, yeah," Torinn responded. "We've been put into something before we could make a choice. So, what's the point in fighting against it? If the good lord Pelor says we have to do it, I say we do it." He shrugged.

"So, team suicide then?" Rolen asked.

"It would be an honor to die next to all of you if it means saving the world," I said pounding a fist against my chest. "As long as we go... as a family."

"You're all insane," Rolen sighed. "But I guess I am too then, let's do this!"

"So where do we start?" I asked.

"I think we should start with leaving this place," Ront responded. "Someone help me up and let's get out of here."

"I'll help you up," Lerissa said. "Let's... go home." She smiled.

"As you guys collect yourselves and gather your stuff, you slowly hobble to the giant doorway that you used to come in," Mr. R began. "And as you get to the doorway, a mist begins to form out of shadows..."

"Seriously!" Lerissa groaned. "How many times do we have to kill her?"

"I run up and pull the hammer up and turn back into the giant!" I called out.

"You all watch as Adrik runs ahead of you dragging his massive hammer behind him with ease. He lifts it into his hands and very comically the dwarf stands between you all and the mist, holding this hammer way too big for him," Mr. R said.

"And giant form?" I asked.

"You don't feel any magic in the hammer anymore,' Mr. R responded.

"Crap!" I moaned.

"And out of the mist walks a familiar aasimar paladin," Mr. R continued.

"I'm going to walk past Adrik and call out to her," Liam interjected. "I am Ront, the new champion of the Raven Queen! Stand down, and we will let you live!" He announced, puffing his chest to make him seem larger.

"The paladin walks up, right to you," Mr. R said. "Looking up at you with a straight face. She reaches for her sword..."

"I pull out my daggers!" Liam interrupted.

"And she drops down on one knee and presents the sword to you," Mr. R finished. "Bowing her head, she speaks up. This is a gift from the mistress. She has called me back into this plane to continue my post here defending the anchor." He looked up at me. "And she told me to give this as a gift to her new champion. May it bring down your enemies as your enemy hath done unto you. And she hands you the sword."

"I guess I take it." Liam shrugged looking at me confused.

"As you take the sword, you feel a rush of energy surge through your arm and into your chest. It's a familiar feeling of power you recognize from your death. Something you felt when Reita buried her dagger deep into your stomach," Mr. R described. "This sword was stolen from the mistress long ago. When the previous guardian abandoned her post. And when she slayed you with it, it returned to its home. And now, the weapon that has brought you into a new power belongs to you."

"I wield it around a little bit getting a feel for it," Liam smiled. His uncle reached over the screen and tossed an item card towards his nephew.

"As you wield the sword, which feels very light for its size, you begin to feel the arcane powers spread and sprout out of your back as a pair of jet black wings unfurled behind you," Mr. R described.

"W-what's happening?" Ront asked.

"You grew wings!" I responded.

"As you speak up, Adrik, the aasimar stands up and walks toward you," Mr. R said.

"I tighten my grip on the hammer," I scowled.

"And you, Master Adrik. For wielding a weapon of great evil for a cause of good, the mistress thanks you. But we must ask you to leave the hammer here in the temple. This hammer serves as our only bridge between the heavens and our world. But she hopes that you shall take this in return." Mr. R reached behind to the shelf and grabbed a journal. He handed it to me, and I examined it. The book had a silver cover with reddish purple gems in the corners. When I opened it to the first page, I saw an image of a skull followed by the words

Tome of Clear Thought.

"A book?" I raised my eyebrow.

"She hopes that you will read it and obtain the knowledge inside." Mr. R nodded in response. "And to you, young wizard." He turned to Laura. "The mistress has given this for you to increase your abilities to fight off the evils that are faced against you." And he handed her an item card.

"Thank you," Lerissa said bowing her head.

"And to the druid." She turned to Rolen. "You watch her reach deep into her pack and pull out a tall staff. At the top is a tree with roots spiraling down the staff." Mr. R handed Ben an item card too.

Ben looked over the card. "Staff of the woodlands? That's amazing!"

"Master Torinn," Mr. R said, now turning to Daryl. "She approaches you and kneels before you. She reaches into her pack and pulls out a necklace with a bead dangling at the end. Much like a rosary or a japamala." He handed Daryl a card. "Your goddess send her hopes that this will help guide you." Mr. R adjusted his gaze over to Jacob.

"Oh no." Jake shook his head. "I didn't do anything. These are the real heroes," he said pointing at all of us.

"I do not have a gift for you," Mr. R smiled. "However, the mistress has another need for you... That is if you will come with me in my return to the heavens?"

Gimble looked around at us all. "Well you guys," He smiled. "I guess this is where our paths part again isn't it?"

"Hey, take good care of yourself now would ya?" I said giving him a quick wink.

"Oh, trust me, I won't put myself in danger without you to be there to save me, big guy," he smirked and returned the wink.

"Hey Gimble," Torinn joined in. "Please be careful wherever you end up. I pray to Pelor every night for your safety. It's never a goodbye. Just a see you later," Torinn smiled. Tears began to well in his eyes and run down his face before jumping out of his seat and running over to his brother and nearly tackling him out of his seat.

"Shall we then?" Mr. R asked Jake, holding his hand out for him to take.

"We shall," Jake nodded.

"You five are the defenders of all that is good and living in this world! May the lords watch over you and guide you to greatness." Mr. R recited. "And with that, Gimble and the aasimar begin to disappear in the misty shadows. As they disappear, Adrik, the hammer fades from your hands and reappears moments later in its original spot."

"I guess it was bound to happen," I shrugged.

"Hey Mr. R," Ben said. "What happened to Elfi?"

"You all look around the temple looking for her. But there seems to be no sign of her," Mr. R said.

"Where'd she go?" I asked.

"She had to have run out in all the commotion," Laura said.

"Think she is still here?" Liam asked.

"Well let's hurry out of the cave before she gets herself killed!" I shouted. "And I start running back to the entrance of the cave."

"We all go after him," Laura smiled rolling her eyes. "Don't lose the damn dwarf!"

"You all run out of the cave. The bridge that nearly killed half your party is once again standing. You make it to the cave entrance, and Elfi is still not to be found," Mr. R said.

"Elfi!" Ben started shouting. "Elfi! Where are you?"

"She's gone, Rolen," I said. I put my hand on his shoulder. "We'll find her soon. Our paths will cross again, I promise."

"I hope so," Rolen sighed.

"And with that, we bring tonight's game to a close," Mr. R said.

"B-but we have so many unanswered questions!" Liam complained. "What the hell happened to Elfi? And that whole Reita thing is unresolved!"

"Guess you'll need to ask those questions next week," Mr. R smiled.

'TIL WE MEET AGAIN

Mr. R took in a deep breath and let it out slowly before rubbing his face. "That... that was a lot of emotion and a great game." He smiled. You could see how exhausted he was. Almost like he hadn't slept in days.

We sat in silence for a couple of minutes.

"That was freaking awesome!" I interrupted the silence. "One of the best games in a while!"

"Yeah, Mr. R! That was amazing!" Ben joined in.

"That comes from all of you guys and your role playing. You guys had an amazing game tonight!" Mr. R said. He looked at the watch on his wrist, and his eyes grew large. "Holy cow, it's almost two in the morning. You all better get home before your parents begin calling me."

As he said that, my phone began to buzz on the table.

"Talk about timing," Jake commented.

I picked it up and headed into the kitchen. It was mom calling. I slid to answer.

"Hello?" I said into the phone.

"Hi baby," Mom responded. "Hey, I am on my way to you right now. It got really busy right before I was about to leave and then had me stay another couple hours. I'm sorry I'm gonna be so late. But I'm only fifteen minutes away."

"No worries, Mom." I chuckled. "We just finished up. It was really good tonight! I'm telling you, one of these nights you'll have to join us... Elfi!"

"Ahhh, he told you guys, didn't he?" She laughed.

"He sure did. Although we lost her in a cave and can't find her," I told her.

"Oh man." She giggled again. "Well, I'm about to get on the highway, so I need to let you go," she said.

"Okay, Mama. Drive careful please," I told her.

"I will. You be careful too, okay? I love you," she said.

"I love you, too," I responded. She disconnected the call, and I looked at my screen as it transitioned to the lock screen.

2:04

Holy crap! It was getting late! I went back into the game room. Everyone was packing up their gear and adjusting their sheets.

"Hey, you bum," Liam said to me. "He said we could regain all our hit points and stuff. When we come back, we are gonna jump a couple of weeks."

"A couple of weeks?" I asked.

"Yeah." He laughed. "Maybe you can do a little learning in those few weeks." He punched my shoulder. It didn't hurt like the ones before. "Clean your crap, and maybe we can go listen to Dragon Talk a little before your mom gets here."

"Yeah!" I responded. "I'll hurry up here. She says she's gonna be a little late anyway. She just left work."

"Awesome, I'll be upstairs," Liam said as he ran into the kitchen.

I went over to my spot and began shoveling my dice into my

bag. I picked my backpack up and set it in my chair. I started putting all my things into my bag when Mr. R wheeled up to me.

"Hey bud, great game tonight." He smiled putting his hand on my shoulder. "I just wanna check and make sure you're all good? No asthma attacks? Nothing personal that you need to talk about?" he asked.

"No, I think I'll be okay," I told him.

"Alright kiddo." He patted my back. "Just remember, if there is ever anything you need to get off your chest, I'm here to listen and chat." He started wheeling towards the kitchen.

"Hey, Mr. R," I said. He stopped and turned around. "Thanks for doing all this for us. It's been a great place to come and escape the world the past few years. It's made everything a lot easier and happier. Even my mom seems to be happy again."

"That right there..." He pointed at me. I could see tears well up in his eyes now. "That right there means the whole world to hear." And he wheeled back over to me and pulled me into a huge hug. "Alright, now get your stuff packed. I know Liam is waiting for you to go upstairs." He smiled at me before wheeling into the kitchen.

I began packing my things up again. But then Daryl and Ben interrupted me.

"Hey Jack," Daryl said. I looked up at him in response. "You mind if we come listen with you guys?"

"Oh yeah. Why wouldn't we?" I smiled.

"Cool." He sighed. "See you upstairs then?"

"Yeah, I'll be up in a sec," I told him.

Daryl pushed Ben towards the kitchen. Daryl stopped in the doorway as Ben ran up the stairs. He turned back and signed to me.

Get some from Laura. He laughed and ran off before I could respond. I shook my head and continued packing. But not before Jake and Laura could interrupt too.

"Hey, Jack," Jacob said.

"Yeah?" I grunted.

"Just wanted to say, awesome work tonight," He exclaimed putting his fist out. I bumped my fist with his.

"Thanks!" I smiled. "And thanks for coming and hanging out with us losers on one of your last days of leave."

"I missed playing with you guys." He laughed. "And it's nice to hang with the gang. You all are like my brothers."

"One of us *is* your brother," Laura joked.

"You know what I meant." Jake laughed again. "Anyways, I bet Matt already said it, but I just want you to know. If you ever need someone to talk to, you can always talk to any of us!"

"I will," I said. "And hey, thank you for earlier. I needed it." I smiled. He grabbed me and pulled me in for another hug.

"'Til next time, kiddo," he said to me. He put his fist out for another fist bump. And I obliged. He tousled my hair and headed into the kitchen.

"Hey," Laura said after Jake left. "Same thing. I'm always here to talk."

"I know," I smirked. "And hey, thanks for being cool earlier about everything."

"Anytime." She grinned. "I know Ben can sometimes be a dick. But he's family, and we love him." She laughed.

"Ain't that the truth." I laughed with her. She bent down to eye level with me and kissed me on the cheek.

"I'll see you next week, bud," she said as the tousled my hair too and skipped into the kitchen.

I finally got finished packing. I threw my pack over my shoulders and pulled the straps to tighten them. I grabbed my trash off the table, carried it to the trashcan in the kitchen, and threw it away. Then I went to the fridge and grabbed a bottle of water and an ice cream sandwich. I put the water in my back pocket and proceeded upstairs to Liam's room.

I opened the door and walked in. I loosened my bag and dropped it in the corner before collapsing in a beanbag. Ben and Daryl were sitting on Liam's bed while Liam sat at his desk.

"Took you long enough, grandma!" Liam said sarcastically.

"Sorry man." I shrugged. "I guess the adults think I'm mature enough to talk to."

"Are those gray hairs in your head?" Liam asked. He leaned closer and squinted at my head.

I looked at the door to check it the coast was clear. And then I promptly flipped him the bird.

"Would you start the episode already?" I asked. "My mom is gonna be here any second."

We hope you enjoyed
Gather the Party.
Here is an excerpt from Antony Soehner's next book,
Unite the Party.

UNITE THE PARTY

CHAPTER ONE: MANY GATHERINGS

I stared out the windshield the entire drive. Never looking off at the signs and billboards on the side of the road. Only occasionally reaching down to my phone to hit the next track button. I've had a recent obsession with listening to Elton John.

Mom and I have been cleaning the house lately, and we came across her stash of old cassette tapes and cd books of music from when her and my dad were dating. Elton John, Lionel Richie, Tupac, Meatloaf, Queensryche, David Bowie, Bruce Springsteen. The list goes on and on. But I've come to appreciate all of them.

Lucky for me though, I've got Spotify so I don't have to lug all those boxes in my car to listen to them. I opened my phone and scrolled through the *Number Ones* album by Elton John. I clicked on *Saturday Night's Alright* at the bottom and turned it up.

I started getting into my head space, like I always do on the drive to Liam's. It harder now to fully prep since I started driving myself. I can't check my sheet while I drive. But it also helps me memorize my stats just a bit more.

"Adrik Frostbeard," I started saying to myself. "Level fifteen barbarian dwarf. A hundred and fifty five hit points," I listed off. "Nineteen strength," I stopped and chuckled a little to myself. "Charisma... Nine."

I still get a laugh out of my big, buff, and awkward dwarf version of me. I still can't see me ever being able to wield the axe like Adrik. But at least I can talk my way out of pretty bad situations.

The song began its final piano riff as I reached the gravel driveway that lead to Liam's house. As I pulled up and put the car in park, I sat and let the song finish out before removing the auxiliary cord. I killed the engine and unbuckled my seatbelt. I sat there for a minute. When I was younger I always dreamed about being able to drive to Liam's on Fridays. But I'm starting to miss having Mom drive me. But enough of that.

I popped my door open and hopped out. I went and lifted the back open to grab my bag out of the trunk. I threw the bag over my shoulder, slammed the back shut, and walked to the door.

You could hear someone's phone go off through the open window in the front as I approached the front door and set off the motion sensor door bell. And before I could even make it up the ramp to the porch, there stood Liam in the open door way.

"Wow, expecting much?" I teased him as I pushed past him into the house.

"Oh can it," he responded giving me a shove. "You're the one who has nothing better to do on a Friday night than play games at my house."

I smiled and shook my head. "Isn't that a good thing?" I said walking further into the house towards the kitchen. "So where is he?"

"Who?" Liam asked.

"Your uncle, numbnuts," I shook my head again. "The only reason I like coming."

"Oh cut the bullcrap," he said punching the back of my shoulder. "You know the real reason is so you can keep that fantasy in your head that Laura will still be available and fall in love with you over what ever idea of heroism you can attempt in this fantasy game we've been playing for years. All in the hopes that one day you will both get married and raise geeky children in your own image," Liam analysed.

I rolled my eyes at him, but... he's not totally wrong. I really do like coming to see Laura. Not that I think we're going to get married or anything he just said. But I won't deny that the thought hasn't crossed my mind before. I sure as hell won't admit that out loud.

"Oh shut it," I responded. "Where's he at?" I asked again.

Liam rolled his eyes and smiled. "He went to get more soda. You drank through most of it last week, remember?"

"Hey man, it was really dry last week,"

"Either way, he's at the store."

"Works for me, gives me time to hide this again," I said reaching into my pocket.

"You didn't?" Liam groaned.

"I didn't do a thing," I smiled at him. I pulled out a folded wad of cash from my pocket. "Now turn around. I don't want you seeing where I'm hiding this." I pointed at him and moved my finger in a circle directing him to turn around. Once he wasn't looking, I turned around and opened the dish cabinet. I took the cash and put it under a plate in the middle of the stack.

"Are you done yet?" Liam asked. "You know he doesn't spend any of the money you guys leave him right?"

"Well then what's he doing with it? Saving it for us all to go to college or something?" I asked. "Because he could use that money for a ton of better things. Lord knows you and I aren't getting into any college," I joked.

Liam's phone started to chime again, alerting us someone was at the door.

We both ran over to the door and Liam opened it. And there on the porch stood my man Wade!

"Hey, hey, little dudes! What's crackin'?" Wade asked.

"What's going on Wade? How's work been tonight?" I responded.

"Ah you know how it is man, party full of drunk people here, stoned gamer kids there, over stressed parent trying to feed the sleep over they didn't plan for. Pretty casual. What about you guys? What went down last week?" he asked, raising his eyebrow in curiosity.

"Oh man, you wouldn't believe what we did!" Liam began excitedly. "We've still been searching for Elfi and whatever the hell is going on with this Death's Hand group, but we made it to Dracomear finally to get some answers. We had to sneak in. They don't like outsiders within their walls. So I'm praying to the Raven Queen we survive this." Liam stopped and drew in the missing oxygen that wasn't reaching his head after rambling through all that. "But if all goes well tonight, we should be closer to learning who this Greg guy is."

"Who's Greg?" Wade asked raising both his eyebrows now.

"Oh man, who isn't Greg?" I responded. "He keeps coming up in everything. It all seems to tie back to him. Reita, Death's Hand, Elfi, The Order of Melora, everything!"

"That's brutal dude!" Wade laughed. "What's the plan for tonight? What are you doing in Dracomear?"

"Well according to Torinn, there are answers in the ancient library there. Were searching for anything. Tomes on all of it," Liam added. "We're at a point where anything will help."

"Well how about a little of this?" Wade said as he popped open the red carrying case and slid out seven large pizzas. "I got one cheese, one pepperoni, one sausage, one hawaiian," he paused. "And tell Laura that's totally gross, pineapple on pizza is a sin!" He joked. "One veggie for the Vet, meat lover for the Game Master, and of course, the Jack special," he finished as he slid out all the pizzas and handed them to us.

"Are we your largest order?" Liam asked as he took the pizzas.

"Ya know the crazy thing is, you're my second largest tonight. We have a huge order for late tonight. It's either a frat party or a really exciting business party, but they ordered two of everything. Tonight is gonna pay Kurtis' rent for the restaurant this month." Wade laughed. "Which reminds me, I've got something in my car for you guys," he said as he turned down the ramp and ran back to his car.

He came back up the drive seconds later carrying a paper bag that was wet on the bottom.

"What's that?" Liam asked puzzled.

"Oh man are you guys gonna freak," Wade said with a smile. He handed me the bag and I took a look inside. There were these plastic containers that were fogged over with a thick layer of condensation to the point I couldn't see in them. Under that were two plastic white tubs that were also dripping wet. But that explains why the bag was wet.

"What's all this?" I asked through my confused laughter.

"Well Kurtis has been expanding our place beyond just making pizza lately. He's working on rebranding as a pizzeria and delicatessen. So he sent me with a bag of items he wants you guys to try and tell him what you think!" Wade responded excitedly. "In the two plastic containers are cannolis, rainbow cookies, and pizzelles. And the white tubs are spumoni. That's why the bag is wet. They were frozen, that's why I was racing over here to get to you guys. So get that in a fridge soon. Or eat it all now."

"Wade, this is too much man! Can we send you with some money or something?" Liam asked. "I know Uncle Matt isn't gonna be okay with all this for free."

"Sorry dude, Kurtis specifically said no money on this one. You guys spend so much with us each week and have been for years. He says it's the least he could do." Wade smiled.

"Well here then," I said as I threw my hand into my pocket. I grabbed the twenty bucks my mom gave me and handed it to him. "Your delivery tip, if you wanna share it with him that's up to you. Or keep it, either way you guys deserve it!"

He reached out and took the twenty bucks. "Man you guys are always the coolest delivery I make every week." He smiled at us. "So same time next week my dudes?" he asked shooting us finger guns.

"Oh for sure," Liam and I responded together. He gave his signature over the head, hang loose hand symbol, breakfast club ending walk away. Liam and I laughed and returned the hand signal before closing the door.

"Ok before you make a mess," Liam said turning to me. "Go throw that stuff into the freezer in the garage before it melts all over the place."

"I'll go to the garage with them..." I smirked. "But no promises that it ends up in the freezer." I laughed manically.

"Well if you're gonna be your normal fat self," Liam scowled with a smile. "At least save me a cannoli."

I just smiled and walked towards the garage.

I opened the door from the kitchen into the laundry room and went in and past the washing machine that was aggressively shaking and rumbling. I crossed the room and opened the other door that lead into the garage. I walked down the makeshift wooden ramp made of multiple boards of plywood.

Mr. R's garage had a thick odor of paint and lacquer. This was where his workshop was hidden. There were no cars or bikes in the garage. No camping or christmas gear. In fact, out of all the garages I've ever seen, it was spotless. There were shelves full of painted statues and figures. Up against the wall sat his painting station. A large workbench with rows on top of rows of small paint containers. Cups full of brushes, all different sizes and bristle shapes. In front of his bench sat a tall stool with a fabric strap handle over it hanging from the rafter above.

On his bench he had a what looked like a gruesome looking troll creature sitting in front of a blowing fan.

I walked around looking at his collection of statues. He had everything. There were statues of Batman and Robin. Gandalf and the dwarves, Bilbo and Frodo. Some statues depicted scenes from movies and comic books while some were scenes from his imagination. There was one that I kept getting drawn back to. It was hidden up high on the top shelf. I reached up and pulled it down to look at it.

When I pulled it down a piece of paper fell from under it. I bent down to pick it up, setting the paper bag down. I turned the paper over, I saw a picture. It was a picture of the moment the statue is based off of. It was of my dad and Mr. R when they were younger. I turned it over and saw there was writing on the picture.

Matt and Travis, D&D night

July 15th 20—

The date was smudged at the end. Maybe water damage or something. This was taken back when all our families hung out constantly. Both my parents, Jake, Ben and Laura's mom, Laura's dad, Liam's parents and his uncle with his fiancee.

I've heard the stories from when they were younger. The all nighter game nights, going to Kurtis' pizza shop after getting crazy drunk, all the shenanigans people in their early twenties do.

I could feel a slight knot building in the back of my throat. Looking between the picture and the detailed statue of my father and a younger Mr. R.

"You know, now that I see it, you look a lot like him,"

I jumped and spun around. Clutching the statue a little tighter in my hand. It was Mr. R sitting in his wheelchair. He snuck up behind me.

"You both have the same smile. It's kinda spooky," he laughed. "You alright?"

I became aware of the tears now trickling down my face. "W-what? Oh, yeah. Yeah I'm all good," I sniffed, wiping my tears off my cheek. "All good."

"It's okay to cry bud," Mr. R assured me. He reached out and pulled me into a hug. "I miss him too. Not a week goes by I don't. But it's been getting easier. Because each week I get to hang with all you kids and relive a life that seems so far gone."

I could now feel the flow of tears begin to stream out of my eyes and soak his shoulder.

"Now, don't tell your mom I told you this." He moved me back to my standing position in front of him. "But that was the night your dad and I convinced Jake to drink for the first time... and probably the last!" He laughed through the catch in his voice. "He took his first few shots really fast and ended up throwing up all over your mom. And boy she was not happy about it." He chuckled as he took the picture and examined it. "I tell ya, Jack, I'd give everything to have your dad play with us again. But I get even better now that I have you here. His doppelgänger, his clone—his son. But, you also have some of your mom in you to balance out. Which believe me when I say, that's a really good thing."

Mr. R turned his chair around towards the door. "Now set those silly memories back on the self and throw that bag in the freezer before it melts." He smiled as he opened the door and wheeled into the house.

I turned and put the statue and the picture back where I found them. I picked up the bag, which was now completely falling apart, and quickly ran it over to the freezer. Then I hurried back into the house.

As I made my way back through the laundry room and into the kitchen, I heard both Liam's and his uncle's phone go off with the doorbell alert again. I went to the door and answered the door to Ben and Laura. And Laura's expression said it all.

"You let Ben drive didn't you?" I asked chuckling at her expression of anger and fear.

"How could you tell?" Laura asked, brushing her hair down. "Is it the face of almost dying? The windblown hair? Or the streaks of tears across my face?" She didn't seem as playful about this as I was hoping.

"Calm down," Ben moaned. "It wasn't even my fault. He started going before the light even changed. It turned red as we were in the intersection. You're just lucky I'm as skilled a driver as I am or you wouldn't have a car left!" He rolled his eyes. "Any ways, what's up? Are we the last ones again?"

"Actually," I heard Liam say as he came into the front room. "Daryl and Jake aren't here yet."

And almost like the stars aligned, a large black truck pulled into the driveway. And out got the two brothers.

"Never mind, everyone's here," Liam corrected himself.

"Well, I guess you were right D," Jake said as he walked up the path. "We were late. My bad." He reached into his pocket and pulled out a five dollar bill and handed it over to his brother.

"Thank you," Daryl sang as he took the money. "It's been a pleasure doing business with you." He smiled as he joined the group on the porch.

"Well, quit lallygagging and get in here," Liam said, dragging me out of the doorway. "Pizza's gonna get cold!"

We wandered into the kitchen and Liam started flipping open pizza boxes and putting out plates.

"By the way Laura," Liam said not looking up from his piles of plates he was counting. "Wade says you're gross for picking pineapple on your pizza."

"Eh, who cares, they made it and I'm gonna eat it. What can he do about it?" she responded. "He's not the first, and won't be the last one to tell me his opinion on pizza," she said as she grabbed a plate and pulled a slice from the pie. She didn't even let it hit the plate before she started eating it .

"Easy there slick," Ben said to his sister. "That'll go to your thighs." He laughed.

She set the pizza down on the plate and cocked her fist in the air, jumping at Ben. He quickly jumped away and threw me between them.

"Hey!" I shouted. "I'm not playing human shield in this. You made a weight comment to a woman, now get out here, be a man, and take your punishment," I said as I pulled him out from behind me and threw him at Laura.

"Thanks, Jack," She smiled, and then proceeded to to punch her brother right in the shoulder. He spun around to face me holding his shoulder in pain.

"And for using me as a meat shield," I said to him before punching him in his other shoulder.

"Dude!" Ben shouted at me. I just shrugged.

"Hey, you deserve it," Laura chuckled.

I moved away from the two of them and grabbed my own pizza. I noticed my bag was still on my back when I leaned against the counter. I looked around at everyone and smiled a little. It was nice to think that we have our own group to cause shenanigans with. And it's a mix of blood relations and friendships. But I guess you could call this a family.

Gross, that was a real sappy thought.

"So, Jake," Liam asked across the room. "You've been out of the military for quite a while now. How's civilian life treating you?"

"Oh, uhh," he hummed as he was mid shoving a slice in his mouth. He took a second to chew. Putting his finger up before swallowing. "It's been alright. It's nice to have the ability to come home and get a full-time job with no problem. I'm loving getting to play with you guys each week. Speaking of which, I got a little something you guys are gonna like," he said as he rolled up the sleeve on his right arm. Under the sleeve he showed us a fresh-ish tattoo of a two dimensional twenty sided die inked into his arm, inside the middle triangle was a number seven.

"Why a seven?" Ben asked.

"Well there are seven of us." He smiled looking back at his tattoo. "Figured you guys would wanna see that."

"Dude," Laura said. "That's awesome." She turned around and lifted the hair off the back of her neck. And there on the bend of her neck was the same two dimensional d20. But it was blank. "We kinda had the same idea!"

"When did you do that?" Ben asked concerned.

"A couple months ago," She responded, putting her hair back. "And mom doesn't know so I would like to keep it that way," she said to Ben with a stern look.

He mimed zipping his lips and handing her the key.

"Thank you," she said, accepting the imaginary key.

"Well I think that it's pretty awesome." I piped up.

"Of course you do," Liam mumbled under his breath. I promptly jabbed my elbow deep into his ribs, causing him to groan.

"Thanks, Jack," Laura chuckled giving me a wink. And like it always does, my knees turned to jelly and almost gave out.

Why? Why did my knees always go weak? Everytime she winks at me, talks to me, looks at me! That toothy smile. That soft voice. Those beautiful eyes. You could lose yourself in those eyes. I know I have. But there's more to her than her beautiful looks, so much more. Something about her intimidates you. Not like you stand there in fear she'll hurt you. But that she is powerful. Behind that soft voice, there's force. She could convince both a genius and a meat head to hold hands and think they were married, just by saying it. And that... that power in her voice. That's what get's me everytime. She's just amazing, and I can't wait until she's mine...

"You okay there, Jackie?" I heard Laura interrupt my thoughts.

"W-what? Oh yeah, yeah I'm great! Why?" I asked coming back into my head. Little did I notice that everyone had left Laura and I alone in the kitchen.

"Dreaming again?" she asked smiling. There it was again. My knees.

"Pfft," I scoffed. "No way. I-I was thinking-"

"About us again?" She chuckled.

"W-w-what are you talking about?" I stuttered. "I've never done that," I lied. I could feel the blood rushing to my face.

"Sure, whatever you say." She winked again. "Whenever you're done fantasizing about real life, we're waiting to fantasize in another world." She smiled walking away into the other room.

I sat there watching her walk away before shaking my head aggressively and smacking my cheeks a few times. "Get over yourself! Stop it you bum!" I said to myself. "It'll never happen! You know that!" I shook my head again and pushed off the counter. My bag dropped off the counter and hit my back hard enough to knock me forward a few steps. I grabbed a plate, snagged some more pizza, grabbed a root-beer from the fridge, and darted into the game room.

MEET THE AUTHOR

Raised on a healthy diet of geek and pop culture, Antony Soehner has come to share his love and appreciation for role playing games and geek culture. If it's a random comic book fact, Star Wars obsession, or just the measly obscure movie reference, Antony is there!

OTHER TITLES FROM 5 PRINCE PUBLISHING